Unthreaded

By
Vicki-Ann Bush

Original Cover art by Sorotrax &
final cover design by Dark Angel Graphics

Published By

Faccia Brutta

Dedication

For Karen, Every time you were there at a signing, gave me a shoulder when life had its grip on me, listened as I read paragraphs over the phone, and indulged me in my self-absorption when writing my latest story that had to be divulged, I love you. You are my sister now and forever.

To Samantha, although our friendship came later in my life, I feel I've known you forever. Our connection is one I cherish and will keep close always. My partner in writing crime, you understand the insanity that is me and you still answer the phone. I look forward to the future and the journey we share in the upside-down world of being an author. There's no one else I'd choose to walk this path with.

"It is never too late to be what you might have been."
– George Eliot

Chapter One

Noah Winston squinted. He had thrown his sunglasses in the back of the car and forgot to retrieve them before leaving Travis's house. Just about everyone in Las Vegas knew the intensity of the desert sun made shades a must. He glanced back to a bare seat. *Damn, they must've fallen on the floor.* He'd have to wait it out. Lucky for him, the orange and gold smear across the horizon would soon fall behind mountains, ushering in the shade of night.

His mind wandered to the new video game *Strike Down*, which he'd been playing with Travis. Killing zombies never got old. He wished he had more time for fun and less reality lately. Taking in a deep breath, he sighed. So much had changed in the past year and growing up was starting to feel more like growing old.

Boom! Flap—flap—flap!

"Crap." Noah peered into his rear-view mirror. He turned his car down a side street and parked along the curb. In the distance, the middle school sat sleepy under the canopy of the darkening sky.

Noah adjusted his shoulders. Some memories are better left locked away.

He shivered, his breath escaping in white puffs as he pulled the jack from the trunk of his green Honda. Peering up, shades of purple and sapphire indicated urgency. The dim, amber lighting from the sparingly placed streetlamps wasn't going to make it easy changing a tire after dark.

His nostrils flared as he followed the trail of burnt rubber to the front passenger side of the car and the shredded remains of rubber clinging to the rim. Noah placed the jack underneath and pumped the lever. The tire came off without a battle and in minutes he'd tightened the last lug nut on the spare.

He threw the jack into the trunk, and slammed the lid shut. Tossing his keys back and forth between his hands, they slipped through his fingers and fell to the asphalt. As he bent down to pick them up, he was interrupted by a loud shriek. Spinning around his hand slammed down on the cool black top to hold his balance. Noah stood up, tilted his head, and strained his eyes. Folded in a fetal position in the middle of the road, the stranger rolled back and forth in agony.

Gingerly, he approached. "What the hell?"

The stranger's chin-length hair stuck to his stubbly cheeks as he flopped violently on the asphalt, the whites of his eyes glistening like orbs of glass in the weakening light. Noah's spine stiffened as the young man's faded blue shirt and burlap trousers hardened and turned to dust.

"Oh god, oh god." Noah scrambled to the ground beside him.

Drool trickled from the stranger's cracked lips as he responded with a deep serenade of moans.

"Dude, can you hear me?" Noah waited for a response. "Don't worry, everything's gonna be okay. I'm calling for help."

He dialed 911 and gave the operator their location as he ran back to his car for a blanket.

The young man's clothes had all but disappeared, leaving only a few strips of cloth. Grabbing a flashlight from behind the back seat he aimed the LED toward the desperate young man. The light danced across the black river and Noah took a deep breath to calm his shaking hand.

Sprinting back, he covered the stranger's lower torso with the blanket. Gliding the light over his body, Noah gasped in horror. The young man's skin was suffering the same fate as his clothing. He could do nothing but watch in fear as pieces of skin broke off, floating away in a cloud of dust.

3

The young man yelled out, "Emma!"

"You're gonna be okay, help is coming." Noah looked away.

Paralyzed with fear, he could do nothing but stand by. In minutes the only evidence remaining of the anonymous young man was a trail of grey-brown dust.

The din of sirens speeding toward his location was a confrontation Noah chose to avoid. With no body, there was no emergency.

He grabbed the blanket and quickly ran to his car. Clicking the key in the ignition, he adjusted the rear-view mirror and gazed back one last time before screeching away. When he felt he'd put enough distance between him and the paramedics, he pulled the car over, opened his door and vomited. He sat for several minutes holding the blanket smeared with ash.

Replaying the tortuous death in his head, he couldn't think of any explanation that sounded logical. Every time he closed his eyes and saw the stranger's face fall away, he dry-heaved. Stepping out into the brisk remnants of dusk, he punched two short bursts into his chest with his fist, hoping to calm the frenetic beating. All he wanted to do was get home and collapse on his bed. He drove the rest of the way home in a daze.

Easing the front door shut, he ambled into the kitchen and leaned against the refrigerator. Clutching his gut to hold back the tsunami of acid pushing against his insides, he yearned to lay his throbbing head on the fluff of his pillow. He yanked open the refrigerator door, grabbed a beer, and went up to bed.

He didn't stop to check on his dad or ask his mom about the doctor's appointment. It could wait until morning; all he wanted was a dark room and the weight of a billowy comforter.

Peeling off his clothes, he left them where they landed and took a long swig of beer. Setting the bottle on his bedside table, he crawled into bed and hunkered down under the covers. Closing his eyes, Noah tried to block out the last few hours. But as he drifted, he heard the rantings of the dying young man. *Who is Emma?*

Luckily his busy day at work also kept Noah's mind on track. Selling clothes at the teen favorite, Fearless, he had little time to review the events of the night before. Unfortunately, as he walked out to the parking lot after his shift, the horror came crashing back in.

Traveling up Charleston Boulevard, he shuddered.

When he passed the side street he had veered down the previous night, the pull was too strong. Instead of going straight to his friend's, he felt the car turn, bringing him back to the scene of despair.

He pulled over and shut off the engine. He knew what he'd seen, but it just didn't make any sense. People just didn't fade away to dust. He put his head in his hands and took a deep breath. Was he going crazy? He'd been under an enormous amount of stress these last few months; maybe he finally snapped. But when he glanced at the back seat, there was the evidence. Still covered with gray ash and crumpled, the blanket was where he had thrown it. Noah sighed.

The window was open, and the cool breeze stung his cheeks. It was getting cold. The sky had its last flecks of orange and red, and the darkness was beginning to creep out, capturing everything in its path.

The ignition hesitated when he turned the key. His transmission was growing tired. It just needed to hold on a few more months, long enough for his savings to reach optimum capacity. He cocked his head and observed the side mirror. No cars coming, just a pack of teens dashing across the front lawn of an unsuspecting homeowner. They abruptly darted into the street and ran from the middle school.

Shades of grey, pale blue, and white caught his attention. Leaning out the window, he studied the teens as they raced down the block. Their clothing bore a striking resemblance to the young man's outfit from the night before.

"What the hell?" Noah sprinted from the car and followed them.

Carrying well-rounded sacks, the three boys and one girl were faster than anyone Noah had ever seen.

"Hey!" he called out.

The four strangers peered over their shoulders but continued to run. Gaining momentum, Noah tried to close the distance between them.

"Wait!"

Abruptly the girl halted and turned around. She put up her hand in a stop motion, and Noah eased back.

She was beautiful. Her long, chestnut locks flowed from the bottom of a simple white cap, framing the delicate jawline of her porcelain skin. Her green eyes, like two deep pools of emerald, held a hint of sadness.

He took a step forward, again she raised her hand for him to halt. Standing still, his ears grew deaf from the pounding in his chest. He tried to speak, but the words stuck in the back of his throat.

A light breeze swooshed the bottom of her dress as she quickly turned and joined the rest of the group. Picking up speed, they rushed toward Stewart Ave.

He didn't understand the need that tugged at his soul. She was nobody to him and yet, he had to know her.

They approached the corner. Across the street, a dirt field with the partially constructed First Presbyterian Church stood behind a chain-link fence. The oldest of the four peeled back a portion of the fence and they squeezed through.

"Stop!" Noah yelled.

The girl turned toward him. The faintest of smiles crossed her lips. One of the younger kids pulled at her sleeve, severing her gaze. One by one they leaped through the framework of the door and disappeared.

Noah stepped through the opening in the fence and ran to where he had last seen her. Where could they have gone? He looked out toward the back of the property—nothing. They had vanished.

He sat down and took a breath; this was beginning to become a habit. First the guy last night and now this. What the hell was going on? And why did he feel drawn to this stranger as if he had little control?

He couldn't stop thinking about her. He had to know who she was. As he traced his memory over the past few minutes, he remembered her clothes. They were as strange as the mystery man from the night before.

I need to see Trav, forget what he's gonna think. I need some sanity.

Chapter Two

"Dude, are you sure about what happened? Because I gotta say, this is some weird ass shit you're spilling. I mean, this is like freaky Twilight Zone stuff." Travis leaned against the refrigerator clenching the bottle of beer close to his chest.

Noah rested his elbows on the kitchen island and looked around. The walls were covered in a bright yellow floral paper and the cabinets were painted white with yellow trim. The dishtowels were neatly folded on the countertops with a pattern of yellow and white stripes and the curtains in the window above the sink were a checkered yellow and white with a yellow ribbon to tie them back. Mrs. Morgan loved yellow, she said it reminded her of sunshine, warm and cheery, which was one thing, but this was color vomit.

"I know how it sounds, I hear the words and I half-believe what I'm saying. But it's the truth, I swear. I saw it, all of it, and I have to find out what the hell is going on out there."

"I don't know, how are we gonna check this out? You said yourself there's nothing left from the guy, and the kids disappeared. Sounds like a done deal."

Noah snatched the empty bottle from the counter and walked over to throw it in the trash. "I was thinking maybe we go back out there tomorrow night."

"Go back where? Do you mean the spot you saw the guy or the kids?"

"The kids. We know they're still around, or at least I think they are. We could see if maybe they show up again. I don't know why, maybe it was the clothes, but I think that the guy and these kids, whoever they are, are together somehow. All I know is that I have got to find out who they are, who she is."

"Why don't we go looking for Hoffa while we're at too? I don't think this is a good idea."

"Come on, Trav."

"Okay, tonight we chill and tomorrow we play X-Files and investigate. But I think you should know, if we're going to do this —I'm Mulder."

Noah nodded. "Agreed."

Sober was the preferred and only way to get home and after a few hours of knocking them back, it was about 4 a.m. before he was able to get behind the wheel again.

When he got home, his parents had long gone to bed. Imitating the many ninjas he'd portrayed in various video games, he crept stealthily to his bedroom and closed the door. In the sanctity of his space, he collapsed on the bed and quickly drifted off.

A relentless beep, beep, interrupted Noah's winning battle in his latest dream of zombie terror. Sitting up in bed, he gazed down at the clothes he'd worn the day before. Sniffing under his arms, he winced. He needed to jump in the shower before heading off to work.

Four hours of sleep was not the way to start a shift, but he didn't have a choice. Missing hours was not in his financial plan for a new car.

A quick cup of coffee in his to-go mug and a granola bar had all the ingredients for a breakfast on the run. He gobbled down the bar and knocked back the liquid gold on the ride over to the mall.

He pulled into the employee parking lot, found an open spot and parked. Glancing at his phone, he smiled.

Finally, he was on time for a shift. Life had been rough lately and his diligence with time management had definitely suffered.

Work dragged on and with each stolen glance at the clock, time seemed to stand still. His mother had called during his lunch break to ask if he could pick up his dad's new anti-nausea medication on the way home. Noah agreed. Anything he could do to ease her burden between his dad's medical treatment and her long hours at work was on his list of priorities.

When his shift was finally over, he couldn't get out of the mall fast enough. Whizzing by the glass storefronts, all he saw were blurs of color as he headed for the parking lot and drove straight to the pharmacy. While he waited to be called up to the counter, he stopped at the magazine rack and snatched the latest issue of V Twin. His dad loved anything to do with motorcycles and Noah thought it might be a nice distraction. When he got home, his mom had dinner waiting on the table. He scarfed it down as quickly as he could before yelling good-byes as he flew out the door.

By the time he got to Travis's, the sun was going down. Noah tapped the steering wheel. "Trav, come on get in. We can't be late."

Travis raised a brow. "What do you mean, late? Noah, we don't even know if they're gonna be there. Did I tell you I think this is a bad idea?"

"You did."

"Okay. As long as it's understood that if we wind up dead in the desert somewhere, it'll be all your fault."

Noah rolled his eyes. "You're so paranoid."

"Well one of us needs to be. But we both know the desert keeps its secrets—until it doesn't. Bwahahahaha."

"You're painful, you know?"

When they reached the church, Noah got a better look at the construction site. It was clear the building was nowhere near completion. More framing than walls, the teens couldn't have found refuge in the open space. The doorway that had served as an entrance for the strangers in the darkness only served to add to the mystery. Noah parked the car halfway down the block; he didn't want to spook them if they showed up. It was getting colder as the sun set and Travis started to shiver as they ambled down the block toward the church.

"It's freezing. Tell me again why we had to park so far away?" Travis was rubbing his hands together and then opted to put them in his jacket pocket.

14

"Because I don't want to scare them."

"Dude, you really have to stop watching Shudder. It's freaking you out."

Noah narrowed his eyes and then pointed to a spot where they could sit and wait.

The cold was taking over and Noah could barely feel his fingers when a faint buzz followed by whispers came from behind the church. He tapped Travis on the arm and motioned for him to keep quiet. They came single-file through the tear in the chain-link fence, three boys in their late teens and a girl around the same age. The boys were dressed similarly to the young man who had perished two nights ago. Same burlap pants and a simple button-up shirt. But the girl was the one who captured Noah's attention. Wearing an ankle-length dress in a soft brown with little pink flowers, her hair was tucked loosely under a lacy white cap. Strands of warm brown and sun-kissed red caressed her shoulders.

She was mesmerizing. He wanted to confront them but he was afraid he'd startle them. They hastened down the street toward the middle school, two boys flanking her on either side with the third not far behind.

Noah and Travis hid behind a corner of the building while the four teens entered the school. After a few minutes, they scurried out. Again they held well-rounded potato sacks and kept a vigorous pace in the direction of the church.

Noah's curiosity got the best of him, and as they neared the end of the block he yelled out, "Hey, what are you doing?"

They immediately halted and pivoted to face him. The elder of the three strangers furrowed his brow and clenched his free hand.

"Run! Don't look back, just go!"

Noah shouted, "Wait! Stop, don't be afraid. We just want to talk to you. We won't turn you in, we promise. Just don't leave."

But it was too late. They were already through the fence and had disappeared from sight.

Noah picked up the pace as he and Travis tried to keep up with them, but like the night before, once the strangers crossed the Church threshold, they vanished. Travis searched methodically around the entire area for some hidden entry or underground sewer system, but he found nothing. He finally gave up and sat down beside Noah on a pile of wood planks.

"What the hell just happened? Where are they? Step aside Criss Angel. Mindfreak's got nothing on these guys."

"I know, that's what I tried to tell you. That's exactly what happened last night. It doesn't make any sense. Where did they go? I've looked everywhere. It's just too weird. And why were they stealing from the school?"

"I don't know, but the way they dressed, they're definitely not from around here. *Little House on the Prairie,* maybe, but here—not so much." He blew into his hands. "It's really getting cold. Can we go back to my house and warm up? Besides, I'm starving."

"Always thinking with your stomach. Yeah, let's go."

"What are you gonna do now?" Travis asked.

Noah looked back at the church. "I don't know.

Chapter Three

Travis devoured a ham sandwich while Noah drank a cup of hot coffee before breaking the silence. "I have to go back there tomorrow night. I've gotta know who she is."

"What are you, nuts? You don't know anything about her or them. Hell, we don't even know where they went. It was like they just blipped out of existence. Forget *X-Files*, we're in an episode of *Stranger Things* and I'm not gonna be Barb. We're not dying in the first season. I wanna do things."

Noah rolled his eyes. "Like what?"

"I don't know. *Things*. And like I said—they're strangers."

"I know and that's all the more reason for me to go back. That's the only place I think I'll have a shot at seeing her again."

"Okay, dude, but you're on your own. Being a frozen corpse is not on my to-do list this week."

Driving home, Noah rolled down the window, letting the crisp air sting his cheeks. He couldn't get the girl's image out of his mind. He was drawn to her. There was a pull that wouldn't let go and the more he tried not to think about her, the more he couldn't stop. He had to know her, to speak to her. What the hell was going on? He clenched his chest. His heart thundered with the intensity of a shiny new Lamborghini. He had to go back.

The usual morning ritual faded into an afternoon of errands and the dull two hours of a mandatory work meeting. Anxiously waiting out the remaining time in his bedroom, he was on his feet and out the door at the first sign of the sun's goodbye. This time he hoped for some answers.

He decided to wait near the church construction, hoping he'd get a better view. He was convinced there had to be a hidden entrance to the area that he and Travis had missed the night before. If there was, he'd be ready. He didn't want to frighten her, he just wanted to talk to her and find out who they were and if they had known the guy he had watched die. He was hoping they could give him some information or even an explanation, anything that could help him understand what had happened.

Noah clenched his jaw and briskly rubbed his arms; he should've worn a heavier coat.

His lust for a warmer climate was interrupted by a low hum of voices. Impossible. His eyes hadn't shifted from the doorway to the front of the church and yet, there they were. He remained still and waited to see where they were headed. Again, they set out toward the school. He followed, watching as they cleverly picked the lock to the cafeteria, but this time instead of waiting for them, he went back to the church.

After several minutes, laughter pierced the chill burning the tips of his ears. The teens scampered toward the church and slipped through the chain-link fence.

Knowing this was his chance to make a connection, Noah stepped into view from behind a large boulder. The teens froze, their eyes fixated on him like prey on a hunter. He took a step toward them and they backed away—except for her. She stood directly in front of him. The last glint of light illuminated her stare, creating specks of gold around the deep pools of green. The young woman never wavered as he took another step closer.

"Don't be frightened, I won't hurt you. My name is Noah and I just want to ask you a few questions. What's your name?"

She stood tall. Noah could see she was different. She wasn't afraid.

"You do not understand. We must go and you must not get in our way. Please step aside. This is not your concern."

"But wait, just tell me your name."

One of the other boys grabbed her arm, "Emma, we must leave now. We are out of time. Hurry."

Noah followed them. "Emma, is that your name? Wait, I just want to talk to you. Don't go."

"I'm sorry, it is impossible. We must."

They walked through the framing of the church and disappeared. Noah melted to the ground. There was no reasoning with this, they were just gone.

He felt like a ship drifting in the vast ocean. No direction, no explanation. It was dark now and the debris of the construction took on strange shapes in the shadows from the light of the streetlamps. The moon hung against the backdrop of a black sky, casting an eerie glow that illuminated the mountain in the distance. Noah played the last encounter over in his mind. The more he thought about it the crazier he felt, but then something clicked in his brain. Emma. He had called her Emma. That was the same name the young man kept repeating on Friday night. They had to know who he was.

Now he was even more determined to uncover their truth. He had no choice but to return again at dusk.

Noah took his lunch break in the food court where pizza and garlic knots lured him in with the mouthwatering scent of a crispy crust. Jen Parker, one of his coworkers, was sitting at a table by herself. Noah searched the area for another vacant seat, but with only two weeks until Christmas, the mall and the food court were packed.

She waved her hand to call him over, motioning to the empty chair. Noah did an internal eye roll. He took a deep breath, put a smile on his face and sat down. "Thanks, Jen. This place is a madhouse. I would have wasted half my lunch hour looking for somewhere to eat."

"Oh, don't mention it. Besides my lunch is almost over and I wanted to talk to you about something. I've been trying to get a moment today, hoping the store would slow down for five seconds, but that just didn't happen. I can't believe how crowded it is. Given the way everybody is talking about how bad the economy is, you'd never know it."

Noah looked around the mall. "I know. I thought this holiday season was going to be easier, but no way. It's like people are just getting so frustrated that they're saying, we don't care if we're broke, we're spending anyway. I know my mom is so bogged down with all the medical bills from my dad's treatment we talked about not really doing gifts this year, but my dad got wind of it and that ended that. Credit cards…more like credit trap. Anyway, what did you wanna talk about?"

"It's about this fundraiser we're having at our church. You see, every year around the holidays our church picks several charities to raise money for. We do it by having bake sales, a carnival, selling candy, things like that. Anyway, this year I recommended we do something for the people at the cancer center where your dad goes. You know sort of like a party where they can forget about the fact that they're in pain and having to spend half the day there. We are having an early Christmas dinner at the church for the patients and their families, a few raffle drawings and some activities while they're receiving treatment, so the day won't suck so much, something to help them forget just for a little while. What do you think?" Jen leaned her elbows on the table. "It's this Sunday and I didn't see your dad's name on the list. I was worried your parents didn't get the invite. Could you ask your mom for me?"

"Jen, I don't know what to say. That's a great idea. I can't believe you thought of this for my dad and the others. It gets pretty boring and depressing over there sometimes. My mom hasn't said anything about it so my bet is she doesn't know. I'll ask her later tonight. Thanks for thinking of them."

Jen got up and gave him a quick hug. "You're welcome."

As he watched her walk away, his mind once again strayed to Emma and the others he had seen. He couldn't wait for the day to end.

The house was empty when he got home, and he had a few hours before dusk, so he decided to get some of the chores done that his mom had asked him to do.

Noah emptied the trash and then took the barrels out to the curb for pick up in the morning. He cleaned both of the bathrooms and mopped the kitchen floor and hallway before going outside to rake up the lawn. Vegas wasn't big on colors of the fall, but some of the trees still lost their leaves and the giant olive tree in his neighbor's backyard had spilled over to theirs. When he was done with the yard work he checked his watch. He still had about forty-five minutes, so he decided to start his laundry.

He had just finished putting some chili together for dinner when his parents came home.

"Okay, what's up?" His mom sat down at the kitchen table. "This room is sparkling. What's going on?"

Noah chuckled. "Nothing. I just realized that I've kind of been absent lately and you probably could use the help. I figured I'd tackle those chores you've been bugging me about and do some other things too. There's chili on for dinner and I did the leaves and the floors like you asked. I also cleaned the bathrooms and started my laundry. I'll finish it when I get home later. I'm going over to Trav's for a few hours. He just got a new game and we're gonna give it a try. Will you save some chili for me?" He hated lying to them.

She leaned forward and kissed his cheek. Her tender expression was the best thank you. Noah gave his dad a hug, grabbed his hoodie and was out the door. He felt good about what he had done today and excited about where he was going. He had to remember to tell his mom about the idea Jen had when he got home later. He was sure she would love it.

As he approached the church, he noticed there had been a few changes to the site from the day before. Some of the debris had been cleared and solid walls surrounded the doorway. Noah sat down on the ground and leaned his back against the building.

His mind wandered as he waited for her to reappear, settling on thoughts of his mom and dad. Out of all of his friends, his parents were the only ones who had not divorced. The way they treated each other after so many years made him yearn for the same in his life. Someone he could find solace and comfort with, someone to love, who would love him deeply. He chuckled to himself. As much as he didn't like to admit it, he was a sappy romantic. If Travis could hear him he'd definitely give him a hard time. The way he was feeling about this girl was crazy. He knew nothing about her and yet he couldn't stop. Maybe he'd taken a big step in front of traffic, but he wasn't turning back.

A collective trail of whispers grazed his ear, interrupting his fairytale. He stood up ready to speak, but no one was there. Noah frowned, disappointment gnawing at his gut.

Then, just as before, they appeared from nowhere. His voice held captive by anxiety, Noah struggled to find the right words.

As they crossed the threshold they spotted him. The elder boy held his arm up to stop them from getting any closer, but the young woman ignored his gesture. Slowly she inched toward Noah, bringing a flutter of butterflies to his belly. He squirmed, rubbing his palms on the sides of his jeans. There she was, his desire, standing inches away from him.

"We haven't much time and we must gather some food for our families. Would you please let us pass? We mean you no harm. We just need to move quickly." Her voice melted his heart.

Noah's eyes widened. "You misunderstand, I'm not trying to stop you. I just want to know who you are?"

"Emma! Say no more, we need to go." The older boy grabbed her arm.

"Please, let us go," she pleaded.

"You're going to the school, right? I'll come and help you." Noah's voice cracked.

"No." The older boy moved forward, "You must stay out of this. You do not know what you are getting yourself involved in. Just go and leave us. Emma, now, we must go."

She gazed into Noah's eyes. "I'm sorry."

They darted toward the school, leaving him behind. Bewildered, he followed them. When they reached the cafeteria, once again, they picked the lock. He peered through a small window on the door and watched as they filled burlap bags with food. Noah scurried around the corner of the building and waited for them to emerge. Full bags in hand, they clicked the lock back in place and ran toward the church.

Noah followed them, trying not to be seen. Like the night before, they slipped through the opening in the fence and as they approached the doorway, Noah called out to Emma.

She abruptly halted and turned to face him.

"You'll be here tomorrow night?" Noah asked with anticipation.

"Yes."

"Can I bring you supplies? Then maybe we can talk."

"No, you don't understand. What is your name?"

"Noah, I'm Noah."

"Noah, you have been very kind, but you must not wait for us. You have no idea who we are, and you need not be involved."

"No Emma, *you* don't understand, I'm not going away until I know everything about you. I saw the guy the other night. I watched him die."

"Joseph? You were with him?" Her eyes pooled, tears flowed like a river down her cheeks. She trembled and he reached out to comfort her, but she backed away. "What did he say? Was he in pain?"

Noah hesitated. He didn't want to give her the gruesome, details but lying wasn't a good way to start their introduction either.

"Yes, he was in pain. But it was quick. He kept repeating your name, Emma. He called to you to the very end. Who was he?"

Emma turned her head from him.

"Emma, who was he?"

"He was... my husband."

"Emma, we have to go, now!" The older boy grabbed her hand.

As she ran with him through the doorway, she shouted, "Noah, I'm sorry, I'm sorry."

Noah folded to the ground. A loud crackle lit up the sky, illuminating the passageway to wherever she went. Numbness spread like a fungus through his body. Not even the first droplet of rain cascading down the back of his neck was enough warning to get his tired limbs to move. And as the sky grew angry and the droplets turned into a downpour, he did nothing. He didn't hear the sound of a car door slamming or the slushing of Travis's sneakers as he approached.

"Noah. Come on, dude, you're soaked. Get the hell up and we'll go to my house, you can change your clothes and tell me what the fuck happened," Travis commanded.

"What the hell are you doing here?"

"Never mind, I'll explain when we get to my house."

Noah stood up and walked to his car in a daze. The words repeating over in his head, *my husband.*

The rain eased up about halfway to his friend's house, and Noah opened the window. Breathing in the smell of drenched bottle brush and sage, he let the night take his stress. When they arrived at Travis's, he got out and peered up at the serrated edge slashing through the canvas of midnight blue. A deep rumble shook him to the core, a prelude of things to come, he thought.

They sat in the kitchen and Travis heated up some leftover stew for dinner. Noah had changed into some dry clothes and took a towel to his soaked hair, the whole time reflecting on his moments with Emma. Nothing made any sense. He didn't know anything about her this morning and now, he knew something he wished he hadn't. Her husband had mysteriously crumbled to dust in front of him.

Travis sat down at the table and handed Noah a bowl of stew. "Dude, listen. I went to the library this afternoon and tried to find out some info on your girl, but I don't think you're gonna like what I'm gonna tell you."

"Why'd you do that?"

"I started thinking about them, you know the clothes, the language, their mysterious appearing and disappearing. It was like they were from another time or something. At first, I checked online, but I couldn't find anything. So, I decided to go to the library. You know that section they have of old books on the history of Las Vegas? I thought maybe we'd catch a break. I know it sounds crazy, but everything you've been telling me sounds crazy. You're not going to believe this, but I think I might know who she is."

"Well, who are they?" Noah abruptly got up and paced across the room.

"Around 1879, some settlers came here on their way to California, and because some of them got sick, they decided to stay. They built a little town and were among the first to start the population of Vegas today. You can follow their history for about 20 years and then in 1899, and this is the really weird part, they all disappeared. The whole damn town just went poof, off the map. No more history, not even a mention. It's like they were never here. I started thinking, given the fact that they seemed to come out of nowhere and the funky way they were dressed, it must be them. Maybe they're all stuck somewhere and can only stay here for a little while. That would make sense, don't you think?

31

I mean, that would explain why they're always in such a hurry and maybe why that guy disintegrated."

"Husband."

"What?"

"That would explain why her husband disintegrated."

"Are you serious? She's like eighteen. Are there kids too?" Travis's eyes widened.

"Stop. Trav, I've got to find out what's going on, I need to know more. Will you go with me to the library tomorrow? Maybe you missed something, I don't know, but it's worth a shot."

Travis shook his head. "Okay, we'll go tomorrow morning as soon as it opens. Lucky for you, Egg Works canceled my shift. I'm sleeping in, no 4 a.m. wake up for this guy."

"Yeah, that sucks. But at least you know you're off by three in the afternoon."

"That's me." Travis grabbed his controller off the coffee table and swiftly pounded his thumbs into the buttons, lodging his avatar's axe into the skull of a flesh-eating zombie. "Mr. Lucky."

After a few rounds of killing the undead, Noah drove home exhausted.

Tomorrow would be another day and whatever he found out would be better than the emptiness of being completely in the dark.

Chapter Four

Travis picked him up around ten o'clock and they ran by Fearless to grab Noah's paycheck before hitting the library. Jen was working the register and he flashed a wide grin.

"Hi, Jen. You remember Travis, right? He came with me to your End of Summer pool party."

"Sure. Hi." She twirled her hair.

"Uh…hi. Great party." Travis looked up at the ceiling.

"Thanks. Hey, Noah, Have you had a chance to talk to your mom yet about my suggestion for the cancer center?"

Noah sighed. He'd forgotten to tell his mom. "No, I'm sorry. She's been so busy with Dad and last night was brutal, but I promise I will tonight. I'm sure she'll love it, but after I talk to her I'll give you a call and let you know what she said, okay?"

Jen's gaze dropped to the floor. "Okay, thanks."

The library was hosting a local author reading and the place was fairly crowded.

Travis showed him the section where he had found most of the information, but Noah decided to further his search by asking one of the librarians for help. She took him to a room that contained books that could be viewed, but not checked out. She suggested they search through them and maybe it would have what they were looking for. After about an hour, Noah spotted an entry in a single paragraph in one of the books containing an early registry of the first known settlers to the region. There was a list of names, and just below that, a description of some of the people. One of the main families it mentioned was the Samsons. There was Matthew and his wife Helen. They had three children: Ezekiel, the oldest; Emma, their middle child and only daughter; and their youngest, Henry. Emma was described as having eyes the color of emeralds.

"I found her. It has to be, it describes the color of her eyes Emma Samson, that's her name. I know it. This is her."

Travis scanned the page and then put the book down.

"Now we know who they are. Let's keep looking, maybe we can find something that tells us what happened." Noah reached for another book.

A few hours passed and they were no closer to finding any answers. The raucous growling from Travis's stomach could no longer be ignored and they decided to take a break and run over to Wendy's before continuing their search.

As they sat and ate lunch, Noah couldn't help but gaze out of the window and try to picture what the area must have looked like when Emma's family had first arrived. There had been nothing there, so whatever shelter they had was constructed by them. No one was running to Wendy's for a quick burger. They had to grow and catch the food they ate. It was a life very different than what he knew.

What must she think of the place now? How long had they been able to come through? And from where? Did they watch the town change, or was this something that had happened recently? Imagine being able to see things grow and build up from nothing to all of this. Had it frightened them? Each time they came through something is different. Cars, planes, even the school is huge compared to what they had. It was probably one room...hell, where do they go?

"Hello, earth to Noah. You ready to cut out?"

Noah nodded. "Yeah, let's go. I don't want to waste any more time. Besides, I need to get back to the church before dusk.

The questions are piling up."

The two boys headed back to the library and rummaged through all the remaining books for any additional information. But once again they came up empty—until Travis grabbed the last book in the pile.

"Jesus, Noah, listen to this. You're not going to believe it, but I found something. Here, read this. I think this is exactly what you've been looking for."

Noah grabbed the book and began reading out loud. "In 1879 a group made up of several families from New York set out to find a better life for themselves in California. They had been told of the lush land that stretched for miles, the warm weather and the promise that all they had to do was claim a lot and work the land and they could have a piece of paradise for themselves.

"The journey was long and harsh, much worse than any of them had anticipated, and when half of the party came down with a fever that was claiming them one by one, they made a group decision to settle temporarily in Nevada. They considered themselves fortunate to have discovered the lush green valley planted in the middle of the dry desert and took it as a sign from God that this was their rescue. Time passed, and they grew to love their new home and eventually abandoned the idea of continuing on to California."

Noah paused for a moment. This was her life, her family and friends. "They lived in a community and continued growing over the next twenty years."

"That's it?" Travis leaned over the book.

"Yeah. I mean it mentions the birth of Emma and both her brothers and some other children, but nothing about anything unusual or out of the ordinary. All of this documentation makes it sound like their lives were normal and uneventful. It's just an ongoing account of the births, deaths, and growth of the town."

"Forget *Twilight Zone*, we're in the middle of some *Quantum Leap* shit. The new one. The old one was good, but the new one is better."

"Wait. He leaps into other people."

"Details." Travis smirked.

Noah put the book down in disappointment. They had gotten so close, but just not close enough.

"Dude, wait listen to this." Travis had skipped ahead in the book a few pages. "It's mentioning a story…no, more like a conflict. There was some kind of feud with another group of settlers."

"What? What kind of feud? I thought all the settlers had traveled together?"

"Dude, shut up and let me finish. I was trying to tell you, it's the Legend of Sunrise Mountain, the one right behind my house. Damn. I always liked that mountain."

"What about the mountain?"

"Okay, it says one of the townsmen, James Hanover, pissed off some settlers who had been there for a few years prior to Emma's group. They weren't the sociable kind, kept to themselves and didn't like outsiders. And for whatever reason, they thought the New York group were definitely outsiders— heathens. That's the description they used for them."

"What the fuck? Weren't they all just staking a claim to start a new life? I mean, why bother with stupid crap?"

"I don't know, but I guess they considered intermingling really bad."

"What?"

"This James guy fell in love with Dallen, a beautiful girl with buttery tresses who came from the other group of settlers."

"Buttery?"

"I think they mean blonde."

"That's weird."

"Really?" Travis raised a brow.

Noah rolled his eyes. "Okay, go on."

"The two of them were deeply in love, but her father had already arranged for her to marry another man from their flock."

"Flock?"

"I'm just reading what's here." Travis pushed the book toward Noah. "You wanna read it?"

"No. Go ahead."

"They tried to run away but her father found out and sent some of the boys after them. When they caught up with them, they killed James while Dallen was forced to watch. Dallen lost it after seeing him die and apparently jumped from the side of the mountain to her death. Her father blamed all the settlers from Emma's group. Said they should have stayed back East."

Travis turned the page and shook his head.

"Tell me," Noah said anxiously.

"Emma's father, Matthew, tried to make peace and keep things from escalating. He was like the mayor or something. Anyway, as hard as he tried, they wouldn't listen and started attacking them one family at a time. At first, they would twine mustard plants around spoiled food, and nail it to their front doors in the middle of the night. When that didn't work, things got much worse.

The assholes would sneak into their homes after dark and kill the man of the household, leaving the women and children by themselves to take care of the land. The plan was that if they destroyed enough families, eventually, they'd pick up and go back to New York, or move on to California."

"Are you fucking kidding me?" Noah clenched his fist.

"It was brutal. This other group really believed they were doing what God wanted them to. Like they were the special chosen people."

"Shit."

"The families lost about twenty of their husbands and fathers before something finally changed."

"What changed? What did they do?"

"Well, that's just it, that's when they— disappeared. It says that Emma's dad found a way to keep them safe, but after that there are no more accounts of Emma, her family, or any of the other townspeople. They just weren't there anymore."

"So, if they disappeared, how the hell is their story in the book?"

"There was a kid who managed to escape whatever happened. Settlers passing through found an eight-year-old boy wandering the desert, Thomas Finley.

He's the one who told them what happened. Or at least everything he could remember. He was pretty close to kicking it when they found him. Here's a paragraph on the kid." Travis slid the book over to Noah. "His dad was Matthew Samson's closest friend."

Noah looked at his watch. He had a few more minutes before going over to the church, so he took the book from Travis and started flipping through the pages until something caught his eye. It was a photo of the town in 1898, just one year before they had disappeared. As he studied the picture his heart thundered, pressing against his rib cage and stealing breath from his lungs. There was Emma and her family. Her mother and father and two brothers. That's who the older boy was the other night, her brother Ezekiel. Joseph was in the picture too, standing beside her. She was so beautiful. She looked exactly the same as she does now, one hundred and twenty years later. Noah shuddered as he fought to swallow the acid painting the back of his throat.

That made Emma over one hundred and forty years old. He showed the picture to Travis.

"Dude, how is this all possible? I mean, I know it's real. I'm looking at her picture, but…"

"No more waiting." Noah slammed the book closed. "I'm confronting Ezekiel tonight and he better tell me what I want to know."

"Whoa, okay. And if he doesn't, then what are you gonna do?"

"I don't know yet, but I'm done guessing."

"Alright then. I guess we're headed to the church and whatever happens, I'm there with you."

"Thanks, Trav. I appreciate your help. I couldn't have done this without you."

"I know." Travis smirked and Noah rolled his eyes.

Neither one would admit it, but fear was tagging along on this trip.

They were only a few minutes away from the church when speculation clouded Noah's mind. He turned to Travis. "I wonder how there was so much detail about the accounts of their lives. It seemed very personal, don't you think? I mean, I get the kid being there, but he was only eight. How much would his dad have told him?"

"Oh dude, that's easy. I read that the information had been taken from a journal that had belonged to Emma's dad, Matthew. It was one of the things that had been left behind when they disappeared. I guess it still exists.

Some private collector in town has it. Jon Moreno. He's some sort of big-time antique collector. They didn't mention how he came across the book, just that he let some of the contents be published for historical purposes."

"Trav, if there's a journal and Matthew kept an account of everything that went down, then maybe there's something in there that can tell us what happened."

"Oh yeah, and I'm sure Mr. Moreno's gonna hand it over to us so we can scour through it checking for clues. No, I'm betting your best shot is with Ezekiel and Emma tonight."

"You're right. I just hope we can find out what it is because I gotta tell you, this is driving me completely crazy."

"Yeah, I know, and you're taking me with you."

Noah glanced over at his friend and although he didn't say it, he was glad to have him by his side.

Chapter Five

Noah tapped his foot on the pavement, keeping it in sync with the pumping in his chest. Time was not his friend tonight.

"You know dude, I was thinking," said Travis. "Vegas is really misunderstood. Everyone assumes because it gets so hot in the summer with the temp reaching 110° that the winters are warm too. They don't get it that the night air can get down in the low 30s and sometimes it snows. It's funny to be at the airport in December and watch people get off the plane in shorts and flip-flops only to freeze once they exit the terminal. They should really check the weather before they travel."

"Do you hear that?" Noah whispered.

"I don't hear anything. What are you talking about? It's so damn cold I think my ears are frozen."

"Shh, just listen. It's almost like there's a humming coming from the church."

Travis closed his eyes. "Yeah, I hear it now. Sounds like the intro to Star Trek. Space…the final frontier."

Noah shook his head. "I think it means they're coming." He looked at his watch. "Yeah, it's about time. Look at the doorway to the church and don't take your eyes off of it."

Travis glared at the church. Blackness filled the threshold as Ezekiel came through, and then Emma. A third boy, maybe twelve or thirteen was the last to arrive.

Noah jumped to his feet and hastened toward Emma, but his gait was interrupted by the arm of her brother yanking him backward. Noah stumbled, regaining balance before he hit the dirt.

"Zeke! Stop it!" Emma ran toward them.

"Emma, we have no time for this. We have a job to do. Everyone depends on us. Now we must go quickly. Time is shorter tonight."

Noah realized what he meant. The doorway would close sooner that night. He had less time than he thought. "Emma, please, I just want to talk to you. I know you only have a short time before you have to leave again, but please stay here with me."

"I'm sorry, Noah, I can't. We need all the hands we can get to carry what we need. I have to go." Noah reached out for her arm, but she pulled away.

"Why don't you let us bring the supplies you need? You wouldn't have to go to the school."

"Our father would never allow it. He does not want you involved."

"I'll go," suggested Travis. "I need a few things myself."

"Trav," Noah said in dismay.

"Would you?" Emma blinked.

Ezekiel scowled, but Travis didn't waiver. "You said you need all the help you can get. Well, I've got two perfectly capable hands right here. I'll go with you and Emma can stay here and talk to Noah. Everybody's happy."

Emma turned to Ezekiel. "Please Zeke, let me stay here for tonight. This boy said he would help you. Please?"

Ezekiel started to say no, but the younger boy chimed in, "Yes Zeke, let Emma stay. She deserves it."

Emma turned to him and whispered, "Thank you, Henry."

Ezekiel frowned, then marched toward the school with Travis and Henry following. "Hurry up, we've wasted far too much time tonight." The three boys disappeared as they turned the corner.

Noah motioned for Emma to sit down beside him on a large rock that had been placed as part of the landscaping for the church. For a moment, all he could do was hold her gaze. He wriggled uncomfortably, afraid to say the wrong thing. He decided to play it safe.

"Emma, who's the other boy with you tonight?"

"That is our youngest brother, Henry. He is a very kind soul."

"I'm glad he was here because I don't think Ezekiel would have let you stay with me otherwise. Emma, I need to tell you something. I think I know who you and your family are and why you can only stay here for a short time. Travis and I have been researching your family. We know that your entire town just disappeared in 1899."

"How could you possibly know this?" Emma fidgeted with the string of her cap.

"A young boy who wasn't with you when the incident happened."

"Oh my. Thomas."

"Yes. Some settlers who were passing through found him wandering in the desert. He told them as much as he could remember, but he was pretty bad off when they found him."

"Poor Thomas. He must have been so frightened. He'd wandered off that day and Zeke was getting ready to go look for him. Mr. Finley and my father are best friends. Thomas was like a little brother to us. Did he die that day?"

"I'm sorry, I don't know. That's all we could find out."

Emma peered up to the darkening sky. "This is all so hard to understand. I cannot believe that anyone would spend any time thinking about us."

"Emma, your husband Joseph. He died because he didn't make it back through the doorway in time. Am I right?"

Emma wiped a teardrop from the corner of her eye. "Yes, we only have a short time here before we must return. Joseph had grown more restless with each passing day. He would challenge his time here later each night. That evening he refused to come back."

Noah paused. He didn't want to push her too hard. She was clearly not used to talking with anyone about her family or anyone else from the town. "Emma, where do you go? I mean once you go back through the doorway, where is everyone and why haven't any of you aged?"

"I should not speak about these things. My father would be very angry with me if he knew I was saying any of this to you."

"Please, I want to help you and your family. Let me come with you, I can explain everything to your dad."

"You can't."

"Why not?"

"Once you enter our town, the curse will be on you as well. Noah, you wouldn't be able to remain in your time. You would only be able to come through like we do."

"Crap." He drew a breath to compose himself. "Tell me exactly what happened to you. It's the only way I can help. I'll try everything possible, but I need to know what's going on." Noah pleaded.

Her voice softened with sadness. "You read about us and the attacks my family and the townspeople endured from the others?"

"The others?"

"Zeke started calling them that after they shunned us. We didn't do anything to them. Two people fell in love, that's all."

"Yes, Travis and I did read about a rift with the different settlers."

"If you read it was everyone in their settlement, that is not completely accurate. It wasn't the whole group at first, just one man. Dallen's father. He ignited the hate within his people. They were different from us in their beliefs, but in the beginning we were able to get along. We did not spend much time together. They stayed on their land and we did the same. But it was civil and when we would pass each other in town, we were cordial."

"Okay, that wasn't in the books we read." Noah ran his fingers through his hair.

"After this man infected the thoughts of his people, my father became desperate. We had already lost far too many of our men and moving on to California or going back to New York was not an option anyone wanted. We had come to call this place home and many of us had been born here. No one wanted to leave." Emma paused. Peering up at the mountain she sighed. "My father was told of this elderly man who was a magician of sorts. He could do things, strange things. Everyone in town had given up all hope of ending the horrors we were enduring and had fallen into complete despair. My father sought out this man and begged him to assist us. At first, it seemed as if he was going to help us," she explained. "It wasn't until later that my father found out that the man was Dallen's grandfather.

His heart was black with vengeance for our people. On the day of the end, one of our people recognized him, but it was too late."

"By 'the end,' do you mean your existence in this world?"

Emma nodded in agreement. "He had tricked my father into believing he could save us. He told him to gather everyone in our community and bring them to the center of town; he would place a protective spell on us. With this spell, no one else could be killed or hurt. It would act like a shield and everything would go back to normal."

"And your dad believed him?"

"You have to understand, my father was desperate for help. He had already lost too many of his friends." Emma swiped a tear from her cheek.

"I'm so sorry."

"He would do anything to help them, even if it meant doing something that was in direct conflict with his beliefs and his God. He did as he was told and brought everyone to the center of town, every man, woman, and child. Thomas would have been there too if he hadn't wandered off. My father is a good man, Noah. Everyone trusted him. He just made a very bad choice."

"Can you tell me what you remember about that day after everyone gathered in town?"

"It was about noon. The sun was very warm that day and we were all getting a little heated. My father tried to reassure everyone, telling them everything would be over soon, and we could have our lives and our town back. But he was wrong.

"The old man came and stood on the top of one of the water barrels about fifty feet away from all of us. He was adamant about keeping his distance, and my father did not question him.

"Dallen's grandfather began to chant, and I remember suddenly feeling cold. My head felt very light and I heard an annoying humming in my ears. It became deafening. I tried covering my head with my hands, but it did not work, I screamed in pain and collapsed to the ground and then...darkness. We could hear each other but we could not see a thing. I listened helplessly as children cried and yelled out for their mothers. Henry was calling for my father. It was horrible. Then, as quickly as the darkness came, there was a bright light. We could see the sun again, the town, each other. We thought we were all safe and that it had worked until we tried to leave and go to our homes. We could not pass the borders of the town. We have been stuck there ever since. For us, time just stands still, never changing. Joseph was the one who discovered the walkthrough."

"You mean the doorway?"

"Yes, the doorway. We can only pass through when the sun is setting, and we must be back through before dusk is over or... you have seen what happens to us. We do not know why, and it took the loss of several of our people for us to realize this. We come through each night for supplies. Nothing grows over there; as I said, it is as if time is standing still. My father tries to keep everyone's spirits up, but over the years it has grown more and more difficult. Food has become easier to gather, though. In the beginning, we would steal crops from surrounding farmers. We lost many townspeople because some of the elders refused to eat. They gave their rations to the children. We have seen so much change here, so many things that are very different from what we had once known, and yet we cannot change even the smallest speck of dirt. We are trapped for eternity, and there is nothing that you or anyone can do to help us."

Noah went to reach for her hand but retracted when the pounding of feet to pavement interrupted them. Ezekiel and the others came barreling through the fence with wide eyes.

"Emma, quickly we are nearly out of time. Help Henry." Ezekiel grabbed the food that Travis had in his hands and headed for the doorway.

Noah couldn't let her go, not again. He grabbed her hand.

"Noah, please I must leave."

"I want you to know I'll be here tomorrow night and every night after that. I'll find a way to help you and everyone. I know there's a solution, there has to be. Travis and I will search to see if we can find out any information on the old man's family. Maybe some of them are still here and can help us. We also found your father's journal. It belongs to a man in town. We'll get it. It might contain some information that could help us. Don't worry, and tell them we're trying, and I won't give up."

"Thank you, Noah, I will tell them, and I will look for you tomorrow night."

"Emma, now, let's go!" Ezekiel grabbed her and they disappeared through the doorway.

Noah stared at the empty space where she had stood just a moment ago. No matter what they faced, he'd keep his promise.

Chapter Six

It had been three weeks since Noah had first encountered Emma and her family, and he was still no closer to saving them than when he first started his search. He and Travis had tried repeatedly to speak with Jon Moreno, the antique dealer who had Matthew Samson's journal, but every time they called his office they were told he was out of the country. The library had been a dead-end too. Nothing more had been contained in the countless books the two of them had gone over and over again. The constant weight on Noah's chest was the fear of empty promises. He'd assured Emma he would find a way to rescue them from their fate, but what if he couldn't?

A ceiling of burnt orange and gold would soon leave, ushering in the false peace of a night sky. Noah's often casual drive was more like a lap in the Indy 500 as he rushed from work to pick up Travis and get to the church. Since he only had minutes each night to spend with Emma, Travis would go and take her place helping Ezekiel and Henry gather food and supplies from the school.

The three of them had just emerged from the doorway as Noah pulled up to the curb. The boys ran off and Emma walked to the edge of the lot with him.

Shyly, she allowed her hand to brush against his and he intertwined their fingers.

"Emma, I know I've been saying this to you every night, but I'll find a way, I will. It's just taking longer than I thought to meet this Moreno guy. Every time we call or go to his office they tell us he's out of the country. I know they're hiding something, but I don't know what. Travis has a friend who, well—has a friend. Anyway, he's trying to locate this Moreno for us, we'll find him. I promise you."

Noah's chest ached. He wanted to take her in his arms and pull her close. Gently, he'd lift her long tresses and nibble the back of her bare neck. He'd move his lips along her velvet skin until he could taste her sweet, plump lips.

"Noah. Did you hear me?"

"Uh…"

"I said, I know you are trying your best and we all appreciate everything you are doing, but I do not want to embrace false hope. Not yet, not until we have something more." Emma inched closer. "It is getting late. They should be back already.

I believe Ezekiel is becoming more daring with his time and it worries me, especially when he has Henry with him."

Noah didn't trust himself. He took a step back.

"Did I upset you?" she asked.

"No. Why would you say that?"

"You moved away from me. If I misunderstood…"

Laughter carried along the vibration of air echoed in the night. The couple was interrupted by the playful banter between Travis and Henry.

"Enough. This is not a party. Father would be very upset if he knew the lighthearted manner in which you were acting, Henry. Noah, will we see you tomorrow?"

"Yes, Zeke but…"

"Noah." Emma had grabbed his arm, much to the dismay of Ezekiel. "I want you to stay away for a while."

"What? No. Why are you saying this?" Noah's stomach churned.

"I'm afraid. What if you cannot ever find a way to help us? It would be better for everyone if we put some distance between us."

"Oh, you mean more distance than living in another dimension? Emma, I don't think we could get any further away than that." Noah sounded angry. He didn't mean to, but he was desperate to hold on to her.

"I do not wish to cause you pain and yet I have. I'm sorry." Emma smiled softly. "Alright, I shall see you tomorrow."

The boys stared at the empty doorway.

"I can't keep doing this." Noah locked eyes with Travis.

"Dude, you were harsh. What's up?"

"I don't know. Maybe because I can't do anything to help her. I don't know what the fuck I'm doing."

"We'll figure it out. I didn't get a chance to tell you yet, but I got a call from my buddy. He's got some info on Moreno for us. He'll meet us now if you want."

"What the hell? Let's go."

Noah opted to let Travis drive to their meeting. Normally no one drove his car but him, but things hadn't been normal lately. He leaned his head against the window. The chill of the glass was a welcome comfort against the throbbing in his head.

"You know Mark for a long time, huh?"

"Yeah. Ever since we were kids. My parents used to hang out with his family and we'd take vacations together and stuff. When his dad left, Mark was only thirteen. I felt sorry for the guy."

"That's rough. I can't imagine not having my dad." Noah looked down at the ground.

"Anyway, he's a good guy. Into some seedy shit but I know he's always got my back and I got his."

"I wonder what he's got for us." Noah cracked his neck.

"I don't know but I was surprised when he said he wanted to meet on the steps of the courthouse. You know, given his history with the local badges."

"Isn't the courthouse near Moreno's?"

"Actually, it's a block away. I guess we'll see our surprise soon enough." Travis smirked.

Jon Moreno's office was in downtown Las Vegas. A very different world than the Strip. The Strip was all glitz and glamor. The larger the casino the better and the money that played and stayed there was a monument to more is better. But downtown still held a little of the old charm from the days when Sinatra and his Rat Pack ruled the desert and people still dressed for dinner and a show. A testimony to what Las Vegas used to be like.

"Did Mark say anything else?"

"He said he had information on Moreno's whereabouts but couldn't tell us over the phone because there was something we should both see."

"Cryptic. Also creepy."

"Yeah. He can be a little dramatic, but that's Mark."

The empty streets of downtown Las Vegas reminded Noah of the cities in his zombie video games. At any moment he and Trav would be overrun by a mob of hungry flesh eaters who'd pounce on the car until they reached their intended meal. He shivered as the thought tickled his spine.

Travis pulled into one of the many empty spots across the street from the courthouse and slipped out his debit card from his back pocket to put time on the meter.

"Whatcha doin'?" Noah crossed his arms.

"Feeding the hungry steel box."

Noah looked down both sides of the deserted street and grinned.

"I'm pretty sure they don't charge after six at night."

"Good point." He put his card back in his pocket. "Look, there's Mark." Travis nodded to a guy sitting on the steps of the courthouse with a Starbucks coffee in his hand.

"He looks like a defendant."

"Yeah. He's always a little disheveled, but that's just how he is."

Noah chuckled to himself when they approached the guy and his shirt had a coffee stain plastered down the front of it.

"Where the hell have you been? I'm on my second cup." Mark took a swig of coffee and wiped his mouth with the back of his hand.

"We had something we needed to do first. Sorry you had to wait. What did you find out? Oh, and by the way, thanks for checking this out. I really appreciate it."

"It's okay. Well, first of all, this guy is definitely not out of the country. He's in Utah somewhere. Not sure what town, but I know he definitely landed in Salt Lake last week. There was an itinerary on his computer, and I was going to print it up, but security came checking on the building, so I didn't get a chance.

"I did manage to see that he was moving around, a lot. Provo, St. George, Ogden, the guy was all over the place. Anyway, I don't know why they keep lying to you, but I do remember seeing a flight home in two days. He lands at Harry Reid at about 10 AM. I'm not sure if someone is picking him up but he had a meeting scheduled at his office for noon. I think that would be your best chance to catch this guy."

Noah sat down next to him on the steps. "Travis said you had something we should see?"

"Yeah. There was a locked drawer, that I, well... let's just say I had a key, okay?"

Noah sighed and put his head in his hands.

"Look, dude, Travis said this was really important. Are you really gonna worry about my methods right now?"

Noah looked up at Travis and then back at Mark. "No. I'm sorry, go on. What did you find?"

"This." Mark held out his hand. The cracked leather-bound book he held had the initials MS inscribed on the front of it.

"There. Look, see the initials. Isn't the journal you're looking for by a dude named Matthew Samson?"

Noah reached out his hand, "Can I see it?"

"Sure. It's yours. I don't want it. I grabbed it for you because I thought it might mean something."

"Thanks, Mark."

Noah glided his fingers over the water spots on the spine. Opening the cover, he gently turned the yellowed pages. Exchanging glances with Travis, he furrowed his brow. Whoever Moreno was, he had some involvement with Emma and her family, and it was time he shared. Two more days of waiting. But at least he had something real he could tell Emma. He could hardly wait until tomorrow. Until dusk.

The house was quiet when he got home. His parents were sleeping and Noah gingerly shut the front door, locked it, and ambled to the kitchen. He grabbed a can of soda and winced as he popped the top. Peeling it back, he took a gulp and headed to his room.

Setting the book down on his desk, he pulled off his pants and shirt, and threw them on the floor. He put the can of soda on a side table and crawled into bed. Instinct gnawed at his brain, telling him to browse through the new lead, but he wanted to wait for Emma. They could read it together.

He threw his arm across his forehead and stared at the ceiling.

His last thought before sleep ushered him into the warmth of Emma's arms was his quick assessment of Mark. He had misjudged the guy, something he'd not do again.

The new ring tone Noah had chosen for his alarm wasn't doing the job. He hit snooze twice before forcing himself out of bed. He dreaded going to work. All he wanted was the day to be over. He ambled into the bathroom and turned on the shower. The water rained down his back and shoulders, loosening his tense muscles. Once he was dressed, he hoped to make a quick exit, but his plans were derailed when he ran into his mom in the kitchen. Her chestnut locks were pulled back in a low bun and she was wearing khaki capris and a round-neck navy t-shirt with matching flats. Her go-to look for teaching second grade.

"Morning Mom, just grabbing a Pop Tart. I gotta get to work."

"Hang on. Can you take this package to the post office for me? This is the third time he's left it for us. It's not ours. It's addressed to a Thomas Finley, c/o J. Moreno. The address is correct but…"

Noah let the cherry tart slip from his fingers. It landed on the floor in pieces.

"You okay?" his mom asked.

"Yeah, just rushing. I overslept. I'll take it this afternoon after work."

"Thanks. Please let them know it doesn't belong to us. And tell them to please stop sending it here. And can you get the broom and sweep up the crumbs? They'll attract ants."

"Sure thing mom."

Noah took the package from her hands and then cleaned up the aftermath of his Pop Tart tragedy. Walking out to his car, he kept a vice grip on the small box wrapped in brown paper. Travis was gonna flip when he told him. He set the mysterious delivery on the passenger seat and drove to work.

Noah was so preoccupied with the latest development in the mystery that was consuming his life, he never noticed Jen come up beside him with a handful of broken belts. The shipment of new inventory was large, and Jen had spent most of the day sorting through the boxes and putting everything away.

"Look at these belts. We're going to have to send almost the whole box back." Jen waited for a response, but Noah didn't budge. "Noah. Hey, are you in there?"

"What? I'm sorry. Did you say something?"

"I said, we're going to have to send most of these belts back. They're all damaged. Where are you today? Is everything okay?"

"Yeah, I'm good. Just a little tired, but everything is fine. Travis and I stayed up pretty late last night playing Death Action."

"Is that the new game that just came out?"

"It is. It's awesome. We didn't realize how late it was until his mom came in and told us, but it was worth it. We're gonna play again tonight." He hated lying to Jen, but if he told her the truth, she'd think he'd gone crazy or something.

"Listen, Noah, I've been wanting to talk to you. I mean, more like ask you something."

Noah tensed up. He hoped she wasn't about to ask him out. He would have to say no and that would make work really awkward.

"I was wondering if you wouldn't mind...if it wouldn't be too much trouble...could you possibly give me a ride to work and back home this week? I'm dropping my car off to the shop in the morning and they said it might not be ready until Friday. I'd ask my mom, but she went to California for a few days to visit my aunt.

It'd only be the days we work together. I can ask someone else for the rest of the time. I know it's a hassle but..."

"A hassle? No, Jen, you're never a hassle." Noah's body relaxed as he breathed a sigh of relief. "Of course, I'll take you home, Jen. Don't even worry about it."

"Thanks. You're a good friend." Jen smiled and went back to boxing up the belts.

When his shift was up, Noah darted out of the store, jumped in his car and raced out of the lot. Not a safe move but the electricity running along his veins fueled his need for speed.

Driving to Travis's house he could barely contain his excitement. He couldn't wait to rip open the box and find whatever treasure was waiting inside. He pulled up to the curb and almost leaped out before throwing the car in park. Running to the front door, he rapped on it repeatedly until someone answered.

"Oh hi Mrs. M," Noah said politely.

Travis's mom opened the door wider and stepped aside to let Noah pass by. A petite woman, her thick, blonde hair cut into the perfect bob looked like it weighed more than she did.

"Hi, sweetie. Travis will be down in a minute. How's your dad?"

"He's okay. I think the new treatment is wearing him out though. It's really hard seeing him lose so much weight. He's always been so solid. You know?"

"I know it's hard, but he's strong. And knowing your mom, she's gonna make sure he has the best doctors. He's gonna be okay. You wait and see. Well, I need to get to the store, please tell them we send our regards."

"I will, thanks."

As soon as the door shut, Travis came barreling down the stairs.

"Sorry dude, I had to get a stupid paper finished for Spanish class."

Noah held up the box and wiggled his wrist. "My mom gave this to me this morning. The mail guy keeps delivering it to us."

"Yeah, so?"

"Look at the name—Thomas Finley and care of, J. Moreno."

"What the hell? How did it come to you?"

"I don't know, but this is getting weirder by the minute."

"Well open the damn thing." Travis inched closer to Noah's side.

Pulling his pocketknife out of his back pocket, he tore a seam along the face of the box. When his blade glided through Thomas Finley's name, the mystery package pulsed, sending a shock wave to his fingertips. Noah dropped the box and swayed like a drunken sailor. Travis quickly took hold of him and helped him to the couch.

"What the hell was that? Are you okay?"

"Yeah. I just feel a little woozy. I don't know what happened. One second I'm opening the box and the next I'm feeling this stab of electricity to my fingers. It made me nauseous."

"Maybe I should try opening it."

"What? No. No sense the both of us going down."

Noah stood up and grabbed the package. This time he felt nothing. He ripped off the paper to reveal a battered and worn wooden box. He ran his thumb along the simple brass latch before popping it up and opening the lid.

"What's in it?" Travis asked anxiously.

"I'm not exactly sure."

Noah lifted out a small golden statue and a necklace.

"It's a little man." Travis reached for the small figure.

"It kind of reminds me of an angel. Look, he's wearing a robe and I think that's a horn he's holding. And look at this necklace. The leather cord looks really old."

"What's that, some kind of pendant?" Travis pointed to the jewelry adorning the worn leather.

Noah studied the small glass orb. "I think that's a bee inside."

"What? Let me see." Travis snatched the necklace from his hand. "Yup. That's a fucking bee."

"This reminds me of that movie about the dinosaurs."

"One Million B.C.?"

"No. The one where they take DNA from the gut of mosquitos to recreate them. There's a scene where they show a mosquito encased in amber."

"Oh yeah, I remember that. It was pretty good."

"What the hell, it was fucking awesome."

"We should watch that again."

"Yeah, when this shits over." Noah placed the relics back in the box. "We gotta go. When we see them tonight, let's not say anything about the box just yet. We don't know what it means, and I don't want to add any more stress on them. Okay?"

71

"I get it. Not a word." Travis pretended to zip his lips.

When they reached the church, Noah put the box in the trunk and slammed the lid just as Emma came through the passageway. He walked to her side and handed her the journal. She held it close to her chest, gently gliding her hand across the front cover. She traced her father's initials embossed into the leather.

"How did you get it?"

Noah smiled. "Let's just say Travis has a friend."

"Did you read it?" Her gaze dropped to the ground.

"No. I waited for you."

"I would like to give it to my father first."

Noah looked down as his foot swished in the dirt. "Okay. Hopefully, when you take it to him he'll remember something in the pages. Something that could help us."

"He will try, Noah. I'm sure of it."

Traveling his gaze from her confident eyes to the ample bow of her upper lip, he longed to kiss her, but instead, he nodded toward the edge of the property. They walked around the corner until they could see the last hint of color on Sunrise Mountain.

Noah didn't want to spend time thinking about what they were faced with. The fact that he couldn't see her more than a few minutes a night wouldn't stop him. All he wanted to do was hold her and feel her close to him. It felt good. No, it felt almost normal. Like they were on a date and afterward he would take her home and walk her to the front door. There he would kiss her, releasing the burning passion and desire held captive in his heart.

But that wasn't what would happen. Rather he would quickly steal one last glance before she would leap into the abyss and out of his world. He would be left standing there in an empty lot with a half-finished building and the promise that he would do everything to get them back. But tonight, in the cool air and the purple sky just for a moment, life was good.

Inching closer, he let his pinky finger brush along hers. A creamy warmth flushed over his insides landing in the center of his chest. Hesitantly, he looped his finger around hers. She gently squeezed and he sighed.

"Noah, would I be thought beautiful for this time?"

"What? Are you joking? You're gorgeous for any time period."

She stepped closer until their sides touched. Wrapping her arm around his, she lay her head on his shoulder.

"Is this alright?" she asked.

He leaned his head against hers. "It's more than alright."

"I wish this moment could last forever." Emma sighed.

"Emma?" Noah whispered. "What was it like when you lived here? I mean, did you like it? What were your days like?"

She lifted her head. "So many questions at once, Noah Winston. Let's see. Well yes, I did enjoy living here. The desert is very different than where my family came from, but it has its own charm and beautiful mix of colors. My days were simple, most of the time I watched out for Henry. For the last few weeks before the banishment, I was busy making wedding plans with my mom."

"You miss him? Joseph, I mean," Noah murmured.

"In a way I do. Every day I think of the pain he must have endured in those final moments and it breaks my heart. But Joseph and I were betrothed to each other by our parents. He was a kind man and my father knew he would take good care of me.

74

We were married hours before the deed that sent us into the abyss. Afterward, we never…Noah, we never lived as husband and wife. I remained with my family and Joseph, although I cared for him deeply, was more like a brother to me than anything else. Honestly, I believe he had affections for another and did the noble thing of marrying me to respect his family's wishes. We shared a deep bond and love for one another over the past century, but neither one of us ever wanted a marriage."

Noah lifted his head and turned to face her. A strand of her hair had gotten caught on the bottom ruffle of her cap and he tucked it behind her shoulder. Trembling, she placed her hand across his heart.

Her cheeks flushed as she placed both hands on his chest and pressed her lips against his neck. Noah's eyes widened. His heart crushed against his rib cage as he slipped his thumb under her chin. Leaning in, his desire was interrupted by a familiar shout-out.

"Time to leave!"

The couple abruptly pulled back and ran for the church. As she slipped from his sight he felt a twinge in the pit of his stomach and the frustration of one more evening lost.

Travis sat down on a large rock, part of Las Vegas's contribution to water conservation. Less green, more granite.

"We need to find out more information on this Moreno guy. Coming here night after night is getting us nowhere. And now with that damn package addressed to him…" Travis narrowed his eyes and stood up. "I mean it. This is getting old. I don't know what we're gonna do, but it better be soon. Ezekiel is starting to get anxious and I think he might try to do something stupid like Joseph did. And we both know how well that worked out."

Noah raised a brow. "What if we use the package to lure this Moreno guy into seeing us? We can say something like, it has his name on it and we just wanna return it."

"Dude, that could work."

"We good?"

"Yeah, we're good."

Chapter Seven

As he lay in bed reflecting on the past few hours, one thing was clear to him: Travis was right. They couldn't keep waiting. He wasn't sure why, but instinct told him they were running out of time. If he didn't move quickly, he'd lose Emma to the abyss forever. Rolling over to his side, he stared at the wall until he succumbed to the weight of exhaustion.

Time seemed to slip through their fingers. Noah had left a message with Moreno's assistant regarding his willingness to return the man's package, but after a couple of days went by with no response, he was beginning to think it was a dead end.

There was only a week left until Christmas, and it was growing difficult for Noah to get the time to see Emma. The shopping hours at the mall were extended for the holidays and no one could get out early until after the New Year. He managed to switch shifts a few times, but it wasn't enough.

He was grateful that Travis still met up with her and the brothers, helping them and relaying messages to her. But he missed her, so when Moreno's assistant finally called with the message that the elusive guy was back in town, Noah immediately texted his best friend with the good news.

It was four o'clock and he just had enough time to pick up Travis before heading over to the church. The temperature had already started dropping and the heater in his car wasn't working. Turning the knob to high produced a cool gust of air and then nothing. He pounded his fist on the dash as if it would set everything right. It didn't. When you're used to the summers of hundred and above, the drop in temperature cuts your skin like a knife.

He was blowing on his hands to warm them when Travis got into the car.

"Dude, are you kidding me? It's like an ice chest in here. Why don't you turn the damn heater on?"

"It's not working."

Travis bent over and felt underneath the dashboard. Clenching his fist, he pounded in an upward motion and warm air flooded from the vents. "Just needed a little adjustment." He grinned.

"What the hell did you do?"

"You must have loose wiring. My dad's truck does it all the time."

"Cool, thanks"

"I hope Emma's father was able to find something in his journal. I'd like to get them through so we don't have to keep coming out here all winter."

"Let's hope he did, and not because your delicate body can't handle a little cold weather."

"That was low. You know how I hate the cold and I've been here every night helping your girl out anyway."

"You're right. I'm sorry, Trav. It's just that I feel so frustrated. I don't know. I can't explain it, but I feel like things are about to get bad. I mean, really bad. A lot worse than what they are now."

"Worse? How could things be any worse? There's a whole damn town trapped in limbo and we have no clue how to get them back. Not to mention the girl you love is one of them and her brother is about to go off the deep end if something doesn't change soon. I really can't see how things can get worse."

"The girl I love?" Noah raised a brow.

Travis snickered, "Then how come every time we go there you wind up staying back with Emma and I have to go get food with Zeke the Grouch?"

"I'm getting information."

"On what, Emma's life in limbo land? Sure. We'll go with that."

"Trav…just shut up."

They arrived at the church just as Emma was emerging from the doorway. Behind her was Ezekiel, but this time Henry was nowhere to be seen. Instead, it was an older man of about forty-five or fifty. He had on the same burlap-looking pants like the boys, but he wore a tattered brown hat with a black coat that came to his knees. He looked lost, more-so than the kids, and twice as cautious. Noah shot Emma a look of surprise and Travis grinned.

"What's the smile for?"

"Don't you recognize him from the pictures at the library? It's Matthew. Emma's father."

Noah studied the man's face. Travis was right. It was Matthew, but he looked older than his picture, which didn't make any sense. None of the townspeople had aged a day since they were trapped.

"Noah, I would like you to meet my father, Matthew Samson."

Noah reached out his hand, but Matthew fell to his knees and collapsed onto the ground.

"Father!" Emma gasped as she and Ezekiel scrambled to his side.

"What's happening? What's wrong with him?" Noah bent down to help them pick him up.

Ezekiel's eyes widened as his gaze traveled from Noah to Travis. He nodded to the boys and pointed at a rock a few feet away.

"Help us get him over to that gibber. He can sit and rest a moment."

"Zeke, dude, what the fuck?" Travis blurted out.

Ezekiel glanced over to his father and then to Travis. His lips pursed and he shook his head.

"Sorry, Zeke."

"It's the trip through the doorway. It's much harder on the adults than the children. That is why it's always us gathering supplies. Some of them have actually died going back to our side. It's as if all the life in their bodies is drained from them. My father has only made the journey once before and it nearly killed him. I fear for his life going back, but he insisted on coming with us tonight."

"Why? What's so special about tonight?"

"I am not sure. He would not utter a word about it to either Emma or myself. He just told us he had to meet you and speak with you."

Noah bent down next to Matthew. "Sir, I know there is something you'd like to talk to me about, but couldn't you have just told Ezekiel or Emma? It seems too dangerous for you to be here."

"No, Noah, I must speak to you alone. Ezekiel, take your sister and go for the supplies while Noah and I discuss some things." Ezekiel knitted his brow but didn't argue. He grabbed Emma's arm and pulled her toward the school obediently.

"Noah, do you want me to stay?" Travis asked.

"Mr. Matthews, this is my friend, Travis. He's been helping me figure out what's happened to your people." Noah peered up at his friend. "Trav, do you mind? I think Matthew just wants to talk with me."

Matthew nodded in agreement.

"Sure. No problem, I'll see you in a few."

Noah fist-bumped his best friend and waited a minute for him to leave before sitting down next to Matthew.

"Okay, Mr. Samson, what is it you wanted to talk about?"

"First, I want to thank you. Emma has told me everything you have done to help them and us and we are very appreciative. But there are some things I feel need to be said.

You and Travis are in danger. Neither Emma nor Ezekiel even know the whole story of what has happened to us. I'm afraid I came here to tell you to stop. We have endured enough pain and bloodshed and we do not want to see two more lose their lives over a mistake I made a very long time ago. My daughter and son try very hard to remain strong and hopeful, but our fate was sealed over one hundred years ago and there isn't anything you or anyone can do."

"That's not true, Mr. Samson. We've found someone who might be able to help. The plan is to see him tomorrow and nothing you say will stop us. There's no way we're leaving you and everyone else in nowhere land."

"Nowhere land? An interesting phrase and quite accurate I'm afraid, but you must listen to me. When that man cursed us, Thayne, he used powers beyond those of this earth. He summoned pure evil to do his bidding. We are doomed. Nothing can save our town, and that is my curse to live with for all of eternity."

"About the curse, do you remember anything about it?"

"I remember everything about that day. Thayne kept chanting one phrase over and over again during the ceremony. It was *sons of perdition*.

One of the other settlers told me it was because those are the souls that repeatedly chose not to follow their way in life. They have no place in Heaven, and they are forever lost. Only able to harm the living by possessing the body of a person who lets them take over, they become—a demon."

"Did you say, demon?"

Matthew nodded. "I will never be able to forgive myself for my foolishness but hear me when I tell you that you must stop. For before long we won't be able to come back and my daughter will know agony far beyond that of being banished between the day and the night. Ezekiel told me he sees how you look at her, that you have feelings for Emma. If this is true, then you must walk away."

"Wait. What do you mean? Not come back? What's happening, Mr. Samson? Tell me so I can help. Look, nothing you can say to me tonight will change my mind so you either help us or go back and let us try without you. Either way, we're going through with this and we're going to talk with that Moreno guy tomorrow."

"What did you say?"

"I said we're doing this..."

"No. Who are you seeing tomorrow? The man you referred to before, the one you said might be able to help. His name is Moreno?" Matthew tightened his jaw.

"Yeah. So?"

"Noah, the man that is responsible for this curse, Thayne, his father's last name was Moreno."

"What are you talking about? He was English. You said so in your journal." Noah's voice was like the sound a dog makes when they're startled. A low growl laced with uncertainty.

"Yes, son, he was English, but he was also half-Spanish."

"What?"

"The loss of his granddaughter was not the only reason he chose to deceive us. His hatred started long before that. Her death was the reason that pushed him to act, but Thayne's hatred was brewing for a lifetime. Moreno, Thayne's father, was a kind man and good to his wife and child, but none of that mattered. His Spanish brothers turned their backs on him because of the treatment they received from the English settlers, and the white people viewed him as an impure outsider.

"Thayne was tormented growing up and it made him bitter and dark. Even after he chose to marry a woman from the English settlement and lived a life dedicated to their ways, he never felt at ease with himself. He was always an unhappy man. It was pure stupidity that I trusted him. I did not know at the time who his granddaughter was. If I had, I would never have agreed to let him help us. Noah, you cannot go to this man. If he is a descendant of Thayne, then evil could very well rule his heart and he could be as dark as his predecessor. Your danger is greater than I feared. Son, you must stop."

"Not gonna happen."

"You children today are very obstinate. If you were my son I would..." Matthew looked up at the sky, the night creeping over the last bit of light. He sighed, "I would be proud that you are so brave and would put so many others before yourself. Your mother and father, are they still with you?"

"Yes."

"They must be very pleased with you. I will not argue with you anymore. I can see it will continue to fall on deaf ears. If you are going to see this through, then there are a few things I must tell you. You...we...are running out of time. I will tell you everything I know.."

When Travis came running up to the church with the others, he saw Noah's pasty white complexion and stiffened. Matthew was whispering a last bit of something into his ear as Ezekiel and Emma grabbed their father by the arms and helped him stand up.

"Remember what I have told you, Noah. You will need to be cautious but swift and we will all be praying for your success. God watch over you and your friend, Noah, and for all of us I hope you are successful in your search "

Matthew nodded as he walked through the doorway with Emma and Ezekiel by his side.

Travis lightly backhanded Noah's arm. "Hey, what did he say?" Noah buried his face in his hands. "Okay, now you're scaring me. Come on, Noah. What the hell did he say?"

"Trav, your dad have any guns?"

"Yeah. A rifle for when he goes hunting. Why?"

"He ever show you how to shoot it?"

"Hunting's not my thing, you know that."

"Okay. We'll find another way."

"For what?"

"Armageddon."

The two of them drove over to Starbucks to grab a cup of coffee and warm up. On the way, Noah explained everything Matthew told him.

"Wait. What do you mean, demon? No such thing, right? Tell me I'm right because I'm thinking we're all screwed. Demons are for Catholics and movies. They make great costumes for Halloween but otherwise just bull. Right?"

"I don't think so." Noah rested his head on his hands.

"Why couldn't it just be your average, everyday serial killer? No. We not only have to save the town but now we're battling demons—for real. Stick a fork in me, I'm done." Travis raised his arms in the air.

"Come on, this is serious. Matthew thinks that Thayne somehow called on one of these lost souls and bargained with them."

"What do you mean, bargained?"

"He must have promised something, you know, made a pact in exchange for the demon banishing the town. It's a demon, dude. It's not going to just do something out of the goodness of its heart.

Hell, I doubt it even has a heart. Anyway, what if Thayne enticed it with their souls?"

"What? How?"

"I'm not sure yet."

"Well whatever Thayne promised this thing, it would have to be pretty big for the demon to come and carry out what he wanted. That's not the worst though."

"Oh, that's not the worst? Good. Cause I thought maybe this was getting boring. You know, maybe we could use a dragon or wizard or something thrown into the mix. Oh no... I know. Next you're gonna tell me that in order to save the town we're gonna have to seek out this demon, and somehow convince it to break the spell. But before that, we have to dig up this old white dude, and use his bones to summon the son of a bitch. Any of that close?"

"Trav, we don't have time for you to be a smart ass. There is one more very important detail to this whole mess that I haven't told you. We have until New Year's Eve to break the curse or the town and everyone in it will die. They won't be able to cross over anymore. Matthew said that the day it happened, when the blackness came over them in those few moments, he heard whispering in his ear. The voice said,

'Through time you will cross. Day after day remaining the same until the year came when there would be no more path. On that day, time would end for all those trapped between darkness and light. The first day of the new year twenty-nineteen. Matthew has never been able to figure out what was so special about that day, but he's sure that will be when the passage closes for good. And with no way to gather food and supplies every one of them will eventually starve to death. The whole town will perish."

"There's your souls."

"Maybe. But it doesn't change what we have to do."

Travis leaned his head against the restaurant window. "I don't even know what to say to any of that. First, we need to make this Moreno guy spill, then you get an ancient Loot Crate with that Thomas kid's name on it, and now, you're saying we also have to battle a demon to reverse a curse to save a whole lot of people from extinction, and all in about nine days."

Noah gazed out the window. "Yes."

"We're gonna die."

Chapter Eight

Moreno's office didn't open until ten o'clock, so Noah spent the morning on the internet researching everything there was on the settler's demons.

Since this nasty ass spirit could be anybody, he needed to approach this demon in a non-traditional way. Fuck, why couldn't this be like the Exorcist? They figure out the beast's name, say it, gain power. Nope. We're just pissing in the wind, he thought.

Going on the assumption that it probably was someone that Thayne once knew, he read as much as he could about the early settlers in Southern Nevada. Migrating from back East, Utah, and California, they all had a similar goal but very different ways of going about it. The stricter, more religious sector often seemed to rely on fear and persecution to get what they wanted.

"Maybe that's why Thayne summoned this demon," he murmured. "He felt they had an understanding. A twisted one, but still, a common bond."

He read a few more paragraphs before leaving to pick up Travis. Nothing explained about the ritual used to call on this evil, and Noah suspected that part was intentionally kept secret amongst their clan. He would have to do more research later.

When they got to Moreno's, there was a good-looking, young guy sitting at the receptionist's desk. He was dressed very professionally in a charcoal grey suit with a black button-up shirt and black oxfords. His red hair was cut short but also made him look younger than Noah suspected he was. The guy was setting an appointment on the phone.

Noah approached the desk and waited. The receptionist's raspy voice reminded him of what he sounded like after an intense Golden Knights game.

"Can I help you?"

"We called about the package."

"Oh yes, you can give it to me."

"We'd feel better handing it directly to him."

"He's very busy. In fact, he'll be flying out of the..."

"I know. He'll be flying out of the country. That's what you people at this office always tell us. Look, you go tell your boss we have something that belongs to him. A journal. I'm sure after he hears that, he'll wanna talk to us."

The guy got up and disappeared through a door behind the reception area. After a few minutes, he emerged and sat back down at his desk.

"As luck would have it, he does have a moment to see you before he leaves."

"Yeah. I thought he might."

"Just go through the door and have a seat. He will be with you momentarily."

The office was fairly large with two rectangular windows stretching from floor to ceiling. A hand-carved mahogany desk with a high-back, black leather chair, was the prominent feature in the room. Completing the set were two smaller burgundy leather chairs. There were several portraits from various Spanish artists hanging on the walls, and a small sculpture of a winged skeleton kissing the cheek of a man sat in the center of his desk. A brass plaque at the base of the unusual figure had the words *The Kiss of Death* inscribed on it.

Moreno entered from a frosted glass door in the far corner of the room and gestured for them to take a seat in the burgundy chairs. He wasn't at all what the boys had expected. Much younger and fit, they had pictured an older man.

His jet-black hair was pulled back into a neat ponytail, complimenting his caramel cheeks, and the golden beam of rays piercing the glass reflected his translucent blue eyes. He noticed Noah staring at the statue on his desk.

"That's a miniature of a gravesite statue at a cemetery in Barcelona. I greatly admired it so I had a replica made." Moreno folded his hands on his desk. "My assistant tells me you have something that belongs to me. Something that appears to have been stolen from my office the other night." He leaned in closer.

"Hang on. First, we have some questions." Noah shifted in his seat.

"You steal my property and *you* have questions for *me*?" He stood up.

"Your property?"

"Yes. My property. Now, where is the journal? It's a very valuable antique and if you have damaged it in any way I'll…"

"You'll what? Call the police? Trav, do you think we should dial for him?"

Travis smirked. "Sure. Why not." He pulled his phone from his pocket.

"Okay. Enough, boys. Put the phone away. You're wasting my time. Do you or do you not have the journal?"

"Well, we have it. But it isn't really yours. Is it?"

"Look. Noah, right?" Moreno

"Yes."

"I don't know what the both of you think you're doing but you have no idea the situation you're putting yourselves in. Now, return the book to me and walk away. Believe me, you don't want any part of this. I know it seems to you like I'm trying to hide something, but that's not true. I'm trying to protect you. If you've read it then you have some idea of what I am talking about. This is very dangerous. I wish I didn't have to be involved, but I don't have a choice. You do."

Noah studied his face. The anguish in Moreno's voice sounded genuine, and for whatever reason he believed the man when he said he wanted to keep them from harm's way.

"Mr. Moreno, I'm afraid it's too late. We know more than you would like to think, and we need your help. We do have Matthew Samson's journal. Actually, we *had* Matthew's journal."

"Wait. Had the journal. What do you mean? Who has it now?"

"Uh, well that would be Matthew," Noah stated.

"Matthew who?"

"Matthew Samson."

Moreno tightened his jaw.

"Okay boys, the joke's on me. Who put you up to this? Was it my stupid brother-in-law? Because this is not funny at all. He knows the situation I am faced with and if he thinks so little of..."

"No. Moreno, it's not like that. We are not making this up. Matthew Samson has his journal, and if you sit down for a minute, I'll explain."

The man hesitantly sat down, rested his elbows on the desk, and clasped his hands.

Noah explained to him how he first met Emma and her brothers, the curse, the loss of Joseph and the connection to Moreno's family.

"Matthew said we have until New Year's Eve to help them. After that, there won't be anything we can do. Please, will you tell us exactly what you know? We haven't much time and they're depending on us."

"I want to believe you, I really do. You have no idea what this could mean to me and my family, but I have to admit I have doubts. I've been fooled in the past. My family has been looking for a cure for generations, but nothing we ever find leads us to the end of all of this."

"A cure? What are you talking about?" Travis questioned.

Moreno turned away. "When my ancestor, Thayne, made the deal with the demon, there was a payment."

"Matthew said something about an agreement. He said the demon must have had a catch. That it would never have done anything to help Thayne without a price," said Noah.

"That's right, there was. Every male in my family has been cursed since that day. We were the price he agreed to pay."

Travis interjected, "Damn. I was right—souls."

Noah glanced over to him and expelled a heavy sigh.

Moreno continued, "That's how selfish and full of hate he was. He agreed to give all of his male descendants to the demon as an offering when they turned forty. In exchange, the demon would make the town suffer for a hundred-twenty years before complete darkness. That's the significance of the date January 01, 2019."

"But why that day? And why one hundred-twenty years? It doesn't make any sense. Matthew had no idea." Noah stiffened.

"My father told me before he died that the girl was killed on January 01, 1899. As for the one hundred and twenty, he said that Thayne wanted them to suffer a hundred years plus the age his granddaughter would've been on her next birthday. I don't think anyone is really sure why, but legend says that is what he asked for. This is just as important to me as it is to you, and more. I turn forty on January twenty-ninth. My father also said that even though the town would be lost it doesn't end the curse for our family. The deal they struck extended to every male descendent born. As long as the bloodline continues, there will be a sacrifice." Moreno dropped into his chair and picked up a framed photo from his desk. "My wife is pregnant with our first child, she's due in two months and we're having a boy. It's not only my life I'm concerned about. It's the life of my son."

"Look, Moreno," Noah softened his tone.

"Jon."

"Jon. I don't know how, but we have to make this right. I know it's dangerous, but I don't care. I made a promise and I plan on keeping it. We'll find a way to save them, but it would be easier if we had your help. I think if we all sit down with Emma and Ezekiel, maybe together we can compare stories and see if there's something we've missed. Sometimes it's the smallest detail, but we have to try."

Jon reached for the statue on his desk and ran his thumb over the dying man.

"I've been trying to contact my great-aunt Joyce, but she's been living in Europe. She's flying home tonight. She's the last of her generation. I'm hoping she can fit some of the puzzle pieces together and possibly point me in the right direction. I'll go see her tomorrow. The both of you speak with Emma and her brother this evening. Persuade them to let Matthew give us back the journal. I have some other books that belonged to my great-grandfather. Maybe we could use them to find something new."

Noah tried to calm the frenetic pounding in his chest. Jon was nothing like he had expected. He couldn't imagine living your whole life knowing the precise time you would die. And the horror of knowing generation after generation of sons were brought into the world only to be gifted with an early demise.

His stomach roiled. There was much more at stake now. Not only the town, but this man's family, not to mention his life.

"I'm pretty sure Matthew will give us the journal after he hears everything you've told us. I don't think he entirely trusts us, but I know he trusts his daughter.

We'll get it back tomorrow night. That will give you time to speak with your aunt and we can meet here on Friday."

"Jon, I need to ask you something." Travis leaned in resting his hands on the edge of the desk. "We've been trying to track you down for weeks but each time we called, your assistant told us you were out of the country. We both know that wasn't true and you've been bouncing around Utah. Why the lie?"

Jon's smile didn't reach his eyes. "I'm not even going to ask how you know that. Things are too serious at this point to worry about your talent for finding out my schedule. My wife knows that I take a few trips a year to Europe for my antique store. I thought it would be easier than telling her I was in Utah trying to track down any new journals or books that might help me and my son."

"Easier?" Travis knit his brow.

"She doesn't know. I've never told her. For years we tried to have a baby and we were never able to get pregnant. I thought I'd spare her the pain of knowing the truth when it seemed children were not in our future. I know I should have said something. Marrying her without telling her how much time we really would have together was wrong.

But I loved her so much and had always hoped I would find a way to break the curse before it was too late for me. And then six months ago the impossible happened. After ten years of negative test results...she was pregnant. Since then I've been searching furiously for any information that might help. I can't risk telling her. The news would devastate her and possibly cause her to lose the baby. There is no other way to save my child from a fate that he had nothing to do with. I have to break the curse."

"But why Utah?" asked Noah.

"After the incident, my family migrated to Utah. In fact, that's where I was raised. But when I turned twenty-one my father told me about the family curse, and I moved here to be close to where it happened. I don't know, maybe I thought being around the area where it all took place would help me find something that could break it. The only thing I was ever able to track down was Matthew's journal. That along with the few books my great-grandfather left was all I've had to really go on. When I realized I needed to broaden my search I decided to try going back to the town where my relatives originally settled in Utah. They were pretty spread out over the state, so it's taken me a few weeks to work through all the cities. My aunt Joyce was my last stop, but as I told you she's been out of the country.

I'll head up in the morning. I pray she has something because if not I'm out of options. Or at least options I'm aware of. Maybe once we compare Matthew's journal to some of the ones from my great-grandfather, we'll find something."

Travis rolled his eyes as he stood up and walked over to one of the windows. "Jon, I don't mean to sound like I'm trying to point out something so obvious, but you had the journal. Didn't it occur to you to compare it to the books you had? I mean, I think that would have been the first thing you would have done."

"Wow, thanks for pointing that out. Why didn't I have you here sooner?"

"I know, right?"

Jon sighed. "It seems someone took the journal before I could look at it. I just procured it the week before it was stolen. Before that, it had been lent to the Museum. I didn't think it would have been much help, but then one of my cousins suggested I read it. He figured there could be something. Some detail that wasn't in my great-grandfather's books. I was still in Utah when it first arrived at the office, so you see—no time."

"Sorry, dude. We were just trying to do everything we could to help them."

"Travis is right, Jon. You didn't see what happened to Joseph. It was horrible. They were desperate and we couldn't think of any other way."

"It's okay. Let's forget about it. We have more serious things to think about. We have a plan. You get the journal and I'll speak with my aunt. We'll all meet here Friday night, say seven o'clock. Okay?" The boys nodded in agreement.

Walking to the car, Noah caught a glimpse of Sunrise Mountain. The peak was barely visible on the distant horizon. A blanket of doom draped over him, draining his strength. His arms dropped to his side and his legs trembled. He leaned against the car door for support.

A heavy whisper grazed his ear. "You will all die."

"Noah! What's wrong?" Travis ran to his side.

"Did you hear that?"

"Hear what?"

"I could swear I heard… never mind. It's passing. I'm okay. Let's get out of here."

When they got to the church, Emma, Ezekiel and Henry were waiting by the fence. Ezekiel walked over to Noah and pulled him away from the others.

"I need to speak to you. I have a message from my father, but he doesn't want Emma or Henry to know. I will stay with you and Emma will go help Henry and Travis."

Noah was disappointed but he knew it must be important or Ezekiel would never ask. He walked up to Emma and let his hand gently glide over hers. She smiled.

"I'll see you tomorrow night?" Noah asked.

"Of course."

He grinned.

Emma reached out and wrapped her hand around his. "Tomorrow."

Noah skipped a breath. "Tomorrow."

Her silky skin glided across his fingers before letting go. After she and the others were out of sight, Noah turned to Ezekiel. He was pacing back and forth. "My father told me everything."

"Everything? What do you mean?"

"Stop, Noah. He told me about New Year's Eve and the inevitable death of all of us. He said to tell you he remembered something. He was reading his journal again and he had forgotten about a man who was passing through town. He was from Arizona, a settler on his way to California. His name was Emiliano.

When Thayne stood up chanting from the barrel, Emiliano was on the opposite side of us chanting as well. At the time my father thought he was joining in with Thayne, but right before the darkness came my father remembers seeing Emiliano raise a hatchet to a large dark figure that was circling around him. My father now thinks that Emiliano was trying to help us. Noah, he also wanted me to tell you not to say a word of this to Emma. He does not want to worry her or Henry. Everyone has suffered enough, and they do not need to know our fate. It will be upon us soon enough."

"Look, Zeke, we'll find a way to fix this. No one is suffering a fate or whatever the hell you want to call it. We need your father's journal back. Tell him we talked to Moreno. He's a good man, not like his ancestor. In fact, he needs to break the curse as much as you do."

Noah explained everything to Ezekiel down to the last detail. He hoped once he heard it from his son, Matthew would trust them enough to understand they might be able to end the curse.

"I will do my best to persuade my father. He can be a very stubborn man when he feels he is right, but I will tell him everything that you have said. Maybe when he hears that Mr. Moreno is just as desperate as we are to end this, he will agree. My wish is to walk freely once again.

105

I can't help but feel maybe this time it will work. It has to." Ezekiel put his head down.

Noah looked down the block and saw Emma and the boys running.

"Hurry, Ezekiel! Darkness is coming. The door is closing." Emma's eyes were wild with fear. Noah jumped to greet her as they whisked by.

"I am sorry, Noah. We have no time."

In an instant, they were gone, and Noah stood there looking at the empty doorway. He walked over and sat down next to Travis who had found a soft patch of dirt.

"What time again are we meeting Moreno--I mean Jon--on Friday night?" asked Noah.

"Seven. Why?"

"I have to get someone to cover my shift. It's so hard to get away. First it was Christmas and now it'll be after holiday sales. The fucking mall is gonna be a mess. I wish everything was over."

"Dude. No, you don't. If it were over we'd have less time, and at this point, we have almost nothing as it is."

Travis stood up. "Come on let's get out of here."

They ambled to the car and Noah opened the door and hesitated before getting in. He folded his hands on top of the roof and propped one foot up on the floorboard.

"I know you're right. I just feel like everything is caving in on us. I sure hope Jon gets some answers from his aunt. I'm running out of ideas and patience."

"Hey. We're gonna do this. We're gonna find a way to break this crap up. Just a little while longer and you'll be able to hold on to her through the night and the day. Now tomorrow night I'll be here even if you can't break away. Also, it's Christmas Eve. The mall closes early, right? Maybe you'll make it."

They folded into the car and slammed the doors shut.

"Nah. That asshole manager wants us staying to clean up the store."

"Well I'll be here, and isn't that what really matters?" Travis wiggled his brows.

"You're such an idiot."

"Yeah, but a good-looking one." Travis flipped down the vanity mirror and ran his fingers through his hair. "Hey, you know Ezekiel and Emma will bring the journal and we will compare it to what Jon finds out. It's gonna work. I know it."

Noah felt much less confident than his friend, but he didn't say anything else. He figured one crazy in the bunch was enough. No use making Travis nuts with his doubt too.

When he got home that night, Noah pondered what life would be like for the townspeople if they did somehow break the curse. How would they get along? The world had changed so much. Then he thought about what Ezekiel had said. 'To walk freely.' That's probably the only thing they all want. As he closed his eyes, the last thought on his mind was of Emma.

Chapter Nine

Travis had texted Noah before heading out the door, trying to reassure him everything was under control. He'd go and get the journal and the two of them could meet up sometime on Thursday. Tomorrow was Christmas and although neither one of them felt like celebrating, they knew the whole family thing wasn't something they could avoid.

He got to the church early, so he swiped on a Spotify playlist and kicked back in his car for a few minutes. Several of the homes running along the street behind the church had their holiday lights up. Travis admired the one with strands of only white. He preferred them over the multi-colored brand because they gave him a sense of calm.

Tapping his hands to the beat on the steering wheel, he abruptly stopped and sat up. In the distance, a jogger was headed straight for him. His back stiffened as he waited to get a clear view—Jen? Damn, what if Emma and her brothers came through right when she was running by the church? This mess was complicated enough without bringing someone else into the mix.

If he could delay her for a few moments, it would be long enough for them to come through unnoticed. Stepping from the car, he waved just as she was approaching.

"Jen. Hi. What are you doing out here? It's almost dark, and it's freezing."

"I could ask you the same question. I'm jogging, how about you?"

"Uh...the same."

"Really. You're jogging? How come you don't have any running shoes on and you're wearing a heavy coat?"

"I like to sweat a lot when I run. It gets my blood pumping. You know, a better workout."

"Travis, I saw you get out of the car.

"I know I lied, but there's a good reason. I came here to..."

"Travis!" Emma came scurrying toward them.

"Gotta go, Jen, it's been fun."

"Wait!" Jen didn't get a chance to finish before Travis was halfway down the street.

When they reached the school, Ezekiel motioned for Emma and Henry to go inside. When they were gone he pulled the journal out from under his shirt and gave it to Travis.

"My father said to tell you and Noah that he prays you are right about Moreno."

"Zeke. Dude. We are. You'll see, he only wants to help. We're meeting him tomorrow night at seven o'clock. Hopefully, he has some more news for us. In the meantime, hold on. We're trying. You're not alone."

Ezekiel managed a cautious smile before dashing to help gather supplies, with Travis at his heels.

Squeezing through the opening in the chain link fence, Travis couldn't shake the feeling of being watched. When they were closer to the church he turned his head from side to side, searching for any unwanted encounters.

"What do you keep looking for?" Ezekiel asked.

"I don't know. I can't scrap this feeling that someone is following us."

"Maybe it is the night. Sometimes its mysteries that can get the best of us."

"Yeah. You're probably right. Okay, we'll be here Thursday. Or at least I know I will."

Emma frowned. "Thursday?"

"Yeah, tomorrow's Christmas."

Henry's eyes pooled as tears rivered down his cheeks. "It's Christmas Eve?"

"Yeah. You guys didn't know? What? The lights didn't give it away?"

"Henry, go wait for us at the door." Emma gently moved him along.

Zeke shook his head. "Where we go, we have no idea what the days are. Yes, we see this light ritual each year and it is very festive, but we can only guess what it all means. Henry is so little, we never wanted to draw attention to what he's missing."

"Shit. I'm so sorry. I blew it."

"Save us from this fate and I can promise you, forgiveness is yours." Zeke faintly smiled.

"Will Noah be able to come on Thursday?" Emma bit her lower lip.

"I'm not sure. He misses you, Emma. I know he would rather be here than anywhere else."

"I miss him too. Will you tell him for me?"

"Sure."

"Thank you."

Scurrying back to the street, he caught a glimpse of a shadow pass by. His body stiffened as he rounded on the possible threat. Darkness had melted over the neighborhood, taking the last remaining glimmer of the day with it, leaving a murky path of doubt and fear.

The streetlight took its cue and flickered on abruptly, adding a layer of uneasiness to his already heightened anxiety. The air thinned, and Travis struggled to draw in a breath.

He took a step toward the car, lifting each leg as if it were drudging through a pool of freshly poured cement. His head grew woozy and he reached for the base of the streetlight, clutching tightly to remain vertical. There were only a few feet left to tackle and he decided it was worth the risk. Letting go of the post, he pushed through the invisible barrier that was holding him back. As he inched his way to the car, he winced. A puff of hot breath on his neck sent shivers down his spine. The smell of rotten eggs permeated around him, leaving waves of nausea with each foul inhalation. Sweat dripped from his forehead and he squinted. Wiping the burn away with the back of his sleeve, he focused on the few remaining steps to the car.

Grasping the handle, the heat pulsed through his rounded biceps as he yanked the door open and collapsed into the seat, slamming the door shut. Without hesitation, he turned the ignition on and floored it. When he was several blocks away he pulled the car over and vomited into the street. He was still shaking when he reached Noah's house. Swaying up the pathway, he leaned into the front door for support and pounded.

A few moments later it swung open and he stumbled inside, nearly collapsing on the floor. If Noah hadn't caught him, his face would have been introduced to the tile entryway.

"Fuck, dude, are you okay? What happened?"

Noah helped his friend to the couch and waited for a response. After a few seconds of deep breaths, Travis recounted the frightening attack.

"Did you get a glimpse of anything?"

"No. There was nothing there. Well, there was something there, but I couldn't see it. The smell...ugh. It was disgusting. Do you think it was the demon?"

"Maybe. We'll have to talk with Jon. Hopefully, he has more information about this thing. I'm not sure what it wanted with you, though. Why did it wait until Emma and her brothers left? I would think if it wanted anyone it would be them. This crap just gets more complicated by the second."

"Whatever it was, I sure hope that's the last time I ever *not* see it again."

Travis left and Noah went into his room to do some research. He reached for his laptop and typed in demons, and religious beliefs of the Southern Nevada settlers. What he got back was several stories of folklore.

One thing they all had in common was the description of a lower-class demon, a bad soul who carried its hate into the afterlife. A thing that constantly struggled to gain more power and recognition. A more in-depth article described their weakness and how to kill them. Thirty years before the curse that banished Emma's family and the town, there was a traveler, a young holy man called Bourbon. He emigrated from Spain aboard a ship that enlisted him for the trip to provide spiritual guidance and ease tension during the long journey. Once Bourbon arrived in the valley, he decided to stay and make it his home.

His first encounter with the demon was with a group of settlers that arrived from California ten years after Bourbon made his home in the desert. He was able to exercise the beast, but the demon returned five years later. After the second battle, he forged a hatchet that was constructed from the bones of a bison, and etched with a sigil of an iron rod. It was said that any evil struck down with the weapon would return to hell. But Bourbon never got the chance to use it. Hearing of this, the demon never appeared to him again. The holy man kept the hatchet and when he died it was passed down to his eldest son. No one had seen it since.

Noah rubbed his eyes. He hadn't realized how tired he was. Closing his laptop, he pulled off his pants and t-shirt. As he slipped under the security of a billowy comforter, the news of this new development weighed heavy on his lids. As they slowly closed, the darkness ushered in a much-needed sleep and a final thought of the missing hatchet.

Chapter Ten

Christmas was a blur. His mom's family came over. They ate, they laughed, they shouted, they went home. Noah was glad though. His head was nowhere near the holiday celebration and the sooner he could speak to Jon, the better he'd feel. Exhausted from doing everything he could to keep up the happy façade, he fell asleep as soon as his head hit the pillow.

In the morning, Noah's sleep was interrupted by the loud hum of the next-door neighbor mowing his lawn. Crap, he thought, he had overslept half an hour and still had to swing by and pick up Jen on his way to work.

He took a quick shower, grabbed a Pop-Tart and ran out the door. Jen was waiting in front of her house with her arms tightly crossed.

"I thought you forgot about me. I tried your cell, but it just went straight to voice mail. Do you think we'll be late?"

"No, we have a few minutes. I'll get us there in time. Here, take my phone and turn it on for me, please. I must have forgotten after I took it off the charger."

"Okay. But get us there in one piece and no casualties."

Noah laughed. "I'll try my best."

"Oh, and you don't have to pick me anymore."

"Jeez, I wasn't that late."

Jen laughed. "My car just needed a quick fix. I can pick it up tomorrow."

"That's lucky."

"Yeah, for my wallet too. Hey, I was jogging the other night and saw your friend Travis. He seemed a little strange. Everything okay?"

"Yeah, that's just Trav. He's a little off-balance sometimes. But he's a good guy."

"Kind of cute too."

"Cute? What are you saying, Jen? You got a thing for Travis?" Noah gave her a sly grin.

"All I said was that he's cute. An observation between friends. Don't go making anything of it. Besides, I barely know him, and he didn't seem to notice me much. In fact, he seemed anxious for me to move on."

"No, Jen. He just had things going on last night. You know, preoccupied. But I know he noticed you because he mentioned it to me."

"What? Really? He told you he saw me. What did he say?"

"Wow. Glad to see you're not interested."

"Noah."

"He said he saw you, that's all. But if you want, maybe after the holidays we can all go to a movie or something? You know, sort of a casual thing."

"Um, really? The three of us?"

"Yeah. We'll just make it a meeting of friends and you two can get to know each other a little better. He's a good guy, Jen, I think you two would probably have a great time together."

"Why?"

"Why what?"

"You said you think we'd have fun together. Why do you think that?"

"Because you're one of the nicest people I know and he's my best friend. Besides, it's like beauty and the beast. He could use a little taming." Noah laughed and Jen raised a brow.

"Alright. After the holidays."

The after Christmas returns weren't letting up, but it wasn't enough to distract Noah from his thoughts of Emma. He couldn't fail her. The agony of telling her night after night that he'd save them had begun to wear down his hope. The closer they got to learning the full truth, the further away she seemed to get.

When his shift was done, he drove to pick up Travis and they went straight to Jon's office. He was waiting for them in the lobby. His wide eyes and sheepish grin sparked excitement along Noah's veins.

"I am glad to see you two. I can't wait to tell you what I found out. My aunt had an attic full of information. I brought some of it back with me. Let's go into my office, I've got everything there."

A box brimming with papers and several old journals sat on top of Jon's desk.

"Apparently Matthew wasn't the only one who kept a journal. There are books here from my grandfather and great-grandfather."

"Why didn't your aunt tell you about these sooner?" Noah was leafing through some of the books.

"She told me she had hoped that I would never have to deal with this. My grandfather, her brother, was very close to figuring out how to break the curse right before he died. We always thought he'd passed away from a stroke, but she thought otherwise."

"What do you mean?" Noah glided his fingers over the cover of a worn leather tome.

"My aunt thinks he faced the demon."

"Then he found the hatchet?"

"You know about the hatchet?" Jon asked.

"I read about it last night. We need that damn thing."

"She doesn't know where it is. He died before she could find out anything else. But there are some mentions of the hatchet in a few of the journals, so I figured we'd go through them and see what we come up with. I also brought the books I already had. Who knows, maybe we can connect some of the dots. My aunt will be leaving for Europe again soon. She wants to remain there for the time she has left. On a good day, she's really quite sharp, but those days are becoming fewer each year. She's left everything here to me. She never had any kids of her own so I'm it. If we don't find what we're looking for, I'll go back up to Utah on Sunday."

Noah grabbed one of the journals from the box and started reading. Travis opted for a stack of papers and Jon went through the ones he had taken from home.

After about an hour, Noah jumped up. "Yes! Listen to this. It's from your great-grandfather's journal. He left it for your grandfather to find shortly before his death. 'Beware, my son, of the Volgeling. They are a group of humans who have sworn service to the demon in exchange for a life of riches. You will know them by the mark they all bear on the inside of their left hand. It is a symbol of the sun with the left half blackened out. It represents the power of the demon they serve, the power to darken the sun.'" Noah blinked. "Block out the sun? I thought the demon could only harm the person he takes over."

"I'm no expert, but whatever happened to me at the church the other night sure felt painful," said Travis.

Jon's eyes rounded. "What happ…"

"True." Noah interrupted. "I think maybe this demon is stronger than we thought. I mean, it's pretty old. Maybe it evolved somehow."

"It's possible." Jon rubbed his temples.

Noah continued. "He says the hatchet is buried somewhere in the mountain of the rising sun. There's a fucking map."

"Dude, that's Sunrise Mountain. The realtor called it that when my parents bought the house. That sucker's practically buried in my backyard. Oh, that's just too creepy. Does he say why he didn't go get it?"

"No. It just stops a few paragraphs down the page."

"That's because he died shortly after he wrote it." Travis held up a single sheet of paper. "This is his death certificate. Three days after his fortieth birthday."

"I think he was going to get it but ran out of time. He also wrote of being followed by something he couldn't see." Noah ran his fingers through his hair.

"Dude! I told you."

"What the hell are you two talking about?" Jon raised a brow.

"While you were gone, Travis had a sort of run-in."

"Run in, my ass. This thing tried to suck the air right out of me."

"Your great-grandfather said he knew it was the demon. He wrote, 'I know this blackness that follows me is the beast. I feel the heat of his breath on the back of my neck and the stench fills my nostrils with the foulest of odors.

I must go into the mountain and find the hatchet. It is the only chance I have to save my son and break this wretched curse on our family. The devil take my ancestor Thayne, for damning his own family to this darkest of fates.' That's where it ends. Your grandfather must have read this, so I don't understand why he didn't go and dig up the damn hatchet."

"I think he did." Jon's fingers scanned the page.

"Why? What did you find Jon?"

"This entry in my grandfather's journal. He writes about the mountain of the sunrise and a map. He was going up the mountain to search for it, but he was attacked on the first day of his journey and barely made it back alive."

"Attacked by who? The demon?"

"No. By a group of men bearing a tattoo of the sun half blocked out on the inner part of their left hands. He was nearly beaten to death. His sister, my aunt, went looking for him when he didn't return the next day. She found him barely breathing and his skin blistered from the heat of the sun.

"He never went back after that. He surmised that the Volgeling were protecting the area and would give their lives to make sure he never got close to where the hatchet was buried. He lived the next few years feeling like a failure to his son.

He wrote, 'I pray that the heavens above can forgive me for the injustice I have brought upon him. My boy's only fault was to be born into a family that has proven itself unable to right the wrong that was done so very long ago. I fear I am damned for not having the wisdom to defeat the beast and its apostles.' That's the last entry in this journal."

"Alright then. We take the map and go up to Sunrise Mountain and find this fucking hatchet. We only have thirteen days, left so we better start now," Noah stated.

"Whoa. Don't be going all Indiana Jones on us. If those guys are out there, then they're probably watching us. And none of us are good with a whip. Or even have one."

"Trav, if that's true, then where have they been? Why haven't we seen any of them?"

"I don't know, Noah." Jon ran his fingers through his hair. "I'm with Travis on this one. I want this just as much as you, hell, maybe more. But we need a plan. Could be they haven't shown themselves because they've been sitting back, watching us to see how far we'd get. You know, no harm no foul. If they saw we hadn't really been able to find out anything, then why give up their hand by showing themselves? No. We need to discuss this and make a plan."

"Forget it. I don't have time to think. They're all depending on me. Emma's depending on me. I can't fail like your grandfather did." Noah heard the words coming out of his mouth and knew it was too late. He had stung Jon and he couldn't take it back. "Look, I'm sorry. I don't mean any disrespect to you or your family. It's just this time I want the good guys to win."

Jon ambled across the room and gazed out of one of three windows. "You know, all my life, for as long as I could remember, I've been living with this crap. And if I have a chance to break this damn curse and save my family, then I'm gonna take it. But I'm not going to let some barely out-of-his-teens boy thinking with his small brain ruin my opportunity. We'll go up the mountain and get the damn hatchet, but we'll do it the way I say. Let's make a plan that includes none of us getting killed. Okay?"

Noah clenched a fist, the frenetic beating of his heart crushed against his rib cage. "I just don't want to waste time."

"And we won't. I'm only suggesting we think it through." Jon's tone softened.

Noah inhaled a deep breath and released it slowly. "Okay. Let's figure it out."

"Do you mind if I follow you over to the church? I'd like to meet Emma and her brothers. Up until now this has been just stories, I'd like to connect with the people," asked Jon.

"They're not good with strangers, so keep it cool. Okay?" Noah raised his brows.

"Agreed."

"I have a question." Travis raised his index finger.

"What, Travis? What the hell is your question?" Jon furrowed his brow.

"Say we don't get killed by the freaky demon groupies and we find the hatchet. How do we call out the goddamn demon to vanquish it?"

"Here demon…demon…demon."

"Everybody in Vegas is a comic."

Chapter Eleven

Travis lay his head back on the seat during the ride to the church. He remembered what it felt like to have that thing breathing down his neck and he wasn't ready for another meeting just yet. He knew they would have to deal with it sometime soon and his palms began to sweat the more he thought about his last encounter. He tried to explain to Noah in detail what had happened, but his best friend was too distracted with their plan to hike up Sunrise Mountain.

"I hope Jon doesn't spook Zeke. You know how he can be," Travis murmured.

"Yeah, I know. But I think it'll be good to have him explain his family's involvement. It might bring some trust back for both sides. Do you mind going with Emma and Henry to the school?"

"No. Dude, anything it takes."

"Thanks, Trav. This would be impossible without you."

"I know." He smirked. "Hey, you think we should tell Jon about the statue and the necklace? He might know what they are."

"I was thinking the same thing. After we have our meeting with Zeke, I'll show him. I still have them in the trunk."

"Good idea."

"And hey, be careful tonight. I know they take small amounts each night not to alert anyone, but eventually something's gotta give."

"I thought about that too. The other night I saw a guy on the opposite side of the quad and thought maybe he could be security. Luckily he went the other way and we were out of there before he spotted us."

Noah swung the car door open. "Oh, I forgot to tell you. Jen asked about you today."

"Jen, really? What did she say about me?"

"Yeah, I was right. You two would definitely hit it off." Noah smirked.

"No. I was just wondering. She is kind of pretty. Don't you think?"

Noah just turned his head and laughed.

Ezekiel was waiting by the opening in the fence when they arrived, and Emma and Henry had already started the trek toward the school. Jon pulled his car up behind Noah's and parked.

Seeing the strange vehicle, Ezekiel yelled out. "Emma! Come back now!"

Noah quickly intervened.

"Zeke, it's okay. He's a friend. He's helping us.." He waved Jon to come over. "Ezekiel, this is Jon Moreno, the man I told you and your father about. We think he found a way to break the curse."

Noah was explaining the details when Emma's scream cut through the night air. She, Travis, and Henry were running frantically toward them.

"Noah, it's them! The Volgeling!" Travis was gasping for breath. "They were waiting for us at the school. We barely got away. We got to go—now. There's about six or seven of them and they aren't far behind. We managed to fake them out because we know the school grounds so well, but it was close. Noah, I felt the thing in the shadows again. It's out there. I know it."

"Zeke, get Emma and Henry back. We'll handle things on this side."

"No. All of you should run now and leave us. I couldn't bear the thought if any harm were to come to anyone because of us," Emma pleaded.

Noah took her arm and stepped closer. "Emma, listen. Zeke will tell you everything. We'll be alright, but you need to go now."

"Noah." She lay her head against his chest. "You can't promise that."

His hand careened down the back of her long locks as he softly pleaded, "Please, Emma. For me? I need to know you're safe. It's the only way I can do what's necessary."

Tears trickled down her cheeks and he couldn't wait any longer. He grabbed her by the waist and pulled her into his chest. He wrapped his arms around her and gently pressed his lips to hers. The heat grew between them as their bodies melted together. Running his fingers through her hair, he brushed away strands from her face. Trembling, she caressed his cheek with the back of her hand. Her velvety skin was intoxicating and he found himself getting lost in her touch, but he knew it was time. Pulling away, he kissed the back of her hand.

"Emma. Go now."

She tried to run but didn't budge.

"Noah! Ezekiel! I cannot move."

"Noah, it's here. It's holding onto her. I smell it." Travis gagged.

Noah ran toward her, but a steely punch to the face knocked him on his ass. As he struggled to get up, he saw them. Three men dressed in black surrounded them.

"Jon. We got company. Look, there's more of them coming through the gate." Noah pointed toward the front of the church property.

Travis picked up a large piece of wood from the ground and slapped it in his hands like a baseball bat. Ezekiel grabbed Henry and pulled him to the front of the doorway and pushed him through to safety.

Jon ran to Noah and grabbed his arm, yanking him to his feet. Then he pulled something from his pocket and placed it in Emma's hand. Squeezing her hand with his, Jon cried out, " Jedediah Smith!"

Emma grabbed her head and screamed before dropping to the ground. Quickly, he pulled her up and started running with her toward the doorway. Ezekiel followed his siblings when two of the Volgeling jumped him, punching him furiously in the back until he collapsed to the ground.

Travis ran to his friend's side and in a blind rage swung at the intruders with his makeshift bat, but a third Volgeling grabbed him by his shirt and slammed him into a large rock.

Noah was fighting his own battle with a relentless enemy, and no one noticed the three men running toward them with guns.

Travis heard the *pop, pop, pop* and covered his head before scrambling to his feet to get a better view. His eyes widened as Jon lay on the ground and Noah furiously threw punches, trying to fend off his attacker. They fired again and the bullet grazed Ezekiel's left arm. A red river stained the sleeve of his shirt as he gripped the wound to control the bleeding. Travis ran toward him to help.

Noah picked up a large river rock and smashed it into the Volgeling's head, knocking him unconscious. Grabbing Emma, he pushed her through the doorway.

"Travis, hurry! Get Zeke through. It's almost time."

He grabbed Ezekiel around the waist and pulled him toward the threshold. They could hear sirens coming and the men began to scatter.

But Travis didn't notice the Volgeling shielded behind a patch of desert plants in front of the opening.

It was the same man that Noah had managed to subdue. He stumbled to his feet just as the two boys were approaching the church. He grabbed Ezekiel and yanked him from Travis's grip before throwing him to the ground.

"It hurts!" Ezekiel screamed.

Travis turned to his new friend, who lay folded in a fetal position, his clothes falling away to dust. "Noah! He's dying. Zeke is coming apart."

"Get him through, Trav! He'll be okay."

Noah ran toward them as Travis grabbed the Volgeling and punched him in the face. The man stumbled backward and fell to the ground. He picked up Ezekiel and pushed him through the gateway. But before he could get clear, the man wrapped his arms around the bottom of Travis's legs and squeezed. Noah gasped, he tried to move quicker but he was too late. Travis yanked to free his legs at the same moment the Volgeling released his grip, sending him propelling backward into the abyss.

The man quickly scrambled to his feet and took off across the back side of the church.

Noah couldn't move. Jon struggled to get up and, holding his stomach, he stumbled over to him.

"What are we looking at? Where's Travis?"

"He's gone."

"What do you mean he's gone? Where the hell did he go?"

"With them. Travis is on the other side with them."

Chapter Twelve

Travis slammed to the ground. Folding his legs to his chest, he moaned. He raised his left hand to the top of his head and pressed down hoping it would stop the spinning. Dry heaving, he struggled to hold back the burning heat in his throat. The paralyzing nausea was only second to the overwhelming fear that he was about to take his last breath.

"Travis. Travis." Emma knelt beside him. "You will be alright. It only lasts for a few moments. Just sit still and let it settle. Henry, go get him some water."

Travis gingerly turned his head toward the shadows surrounding him and the murmurs ringing in his ears. Fluttering his lids open, a sharp ray of bright light forced him to quickly snap them shut. Slowly, he tried again until his eyes could focus. Towering over him were the other townspeople.

Emma grabbed his arm on one side and Ezekiel grabbed the other. She rubbed his back softly and they both held on so he could use them as a brace to stand.

"Wait. Zeke, you were shot."

"I'm okay, little more than a scratch. See." Ezekiel pulled the flap of his torn shirt, exposing his upper arm. "It will take a long time to heal, but it will not worsen."

Emma spoke softly, "Now go slow. We will be here to hold you until you feel strong enough to stand on your own. The sick stomach lasts the longest, but it will leave you in a few minutes,"

Travis waited a moment before slowly shuffling a few steps. His legs wobbled and he stiffened his grip on Ezekiel's arm. As he gazed at his surroundings, it became clear to him the torture Emma's people had endured for the past one hundred years. The bright light that had pierced his eyes upon arrival was concentrated over the town. Stronger than any Las Vegas summer day, the intensity was nearly too much to bear.

Henry came back and handed him water in a small tin cup. The lukewarm liquid had an earthy taste and did little to refresh his parched throat. His vision had begun to adjust and what were mere outlines moments ago became the buildings that represented the center of the chaos. There was a grocery and grain store, a post office, a dress shop, and a hotel. Across the street was a blacksmith and stables for boarding horses. The sheriff's office was at the far end on the left and a quaint, white church stood on the very edge of town.

In front of several of the buildings were large horse troughs filled to the top with water. Travis wondered how that was possible. Ezekiel had told him that nothing changed or grew, which was why they needed to get supplies nearly every night or risk starvation.

"The water."

"He needs more water." Emma nudged Henry.

"No. How is it the water in the troughs are full? Zeke, you told me nothing changes?"

"The water is the only thing that keeps replenishing itself. We are not sure why, but my father thinks it was to prolong our agony. It's a false gift. It nourishes us only to torture us."

"Jeez dude, that is some cruel shit." Travis raised a brow when he noticed some of the townspeople shaking their heads. He leaned into Zeke and whispered, "Did I say something wrong?"

"Your colorful use of words is not something they are accustomed to hearing. They have not been traveling like Emma and I. It will take them time to adjust."

Travis squirmed. "I'm sure I sound strange to you. I didn't mean to offend anyone. I just meant that it's so wrong. All these years of being trapped and trying to survive...I'm sorry."

Matthew stepped forward from the crowd and put his hands out to welcome Travis. "I am truly sorry, Travis, that fate has bestowed this plight on you, but we welcome you, nonetheless. We will try to make your time with us as friendly and helpful as we can. It is the least we can do. My daughter and sons have told me everything you are doing to save us from this agony. We greatly appreciate the danger you have willingly put yourself in for our sake. We will not judge you or what you say. Please feel at ease."

"Thanks, Matthew." Travis looked over at Ezekiel and Emma. "This reaction...I don't know how you could stand it each night. You never look like this makes you sick when you come through, while I feel like I just got hit by a car and then backed over."

Ezekiel put his hand on Travis's shoulder. "The first time we went through we felt just like you. But it was necessary for our survival to keep going. After a time, each pass through became easier. I think our bodies adjusted. It is far more difficult for the adults though. You saw how it affected my father in a way similar to what you are feeling now. But the difference is that for them, it never gets any better. Another cruel part of the curse. The children are forced into being sent for food. It has been difficult for the adults to let their children walk through to the unknown each night. Emma and I have been going through for a long time.

We have been able to adapt to the transition and get our supplies without much difficulty. Henry just started coming with us the past few times. It doesn't seem to affect him much. For whatever reason, the younger you are, the easier time you have walking through.

Travis raised his hand to shield his eyes.

"It's so bright. Is it always like this?"

"Yes. As I said, it never changes."

"I think I'd go insane. Seeing the light so brilliant all the time, never having the peace of a dark sky with stars shining on a warm summer night...I'd lose my head for sure. It looks like it should be warm, but it actually feels a little chilly."

"Tobias, please grab a blanket for Travis," Ezekial instructed.

In the matter of a minute, a small boy was standing next to Travis with a blanket in his hands. He was about eight or nine with curly blonde hair and cherubic cheeks. He had a huge smile on his face. Travis took the blanket and wrapped it around his shoulders.

"Thanks. Tobias, that's a cool name."

"Thank you, sir."

"Okay, well, first of all, you don't have to call me sir. Travis, Trav, hey you, whatever rolls off your tongue is fine. And second of all, how did you get back so fast?"

The boy giggled. "I didn't. I had the blanket wrapped around me."

"I can't take your blanket. Here, let's wrap you back up." Travis went to put the blanket around the boy, but he jumped back.

"No. I will be just fine, sir...I mean Travis. I will go get another. I want you to have mine."

"Well, thank you but I'm feeling warmer already. You can have it back now."

"Please keep it. I want you to have it for helping us. I want you to" Tobias couldn't finish his sentence. He turned his head and buried it into the apron of a woman standing beside him. Travis figured she must be his mother.

Ezekiel leaned in and whispered in his ear. "Tobias is Joseph's little brother."

Travis shuddered. It's so much worse than he imagined. One by one they had watched as loved ones died in complete agony or desperation. The torture these people had to endure had been immense. He now understood why this blanket was so important to this little boy.

It was his way of doing something. He gave his blanket to Travis to help the person he hoped would be able to help them avoid the same torturous death his brother had endured.

"You know, I am still kind of chilly. I think I'll hold on to this for a while, okay?"

Tobias wiped his eyes and grinned.

"Zeke, how about you show me around your town? This way, when I go back with you tomorrow night, I can tell Noah all about it. I think he's probably pretty freaked out by now and if I can seem okay, you know, like it's no big deal, then he'll be able to focus on getting us out of here."

Emma was shaking her head no. "I do not think that is a good idea, Travis. Remember what you felt like when you first passed through? If Noah sees you like that, he will be devastated and blame himself. I think it is best if you remain here. We will let him know that you are well."

"I understand what you are getting at, but it won't work. I've known Noah since we were kids. He'll need to see for himself that I'm okay. You can help me explain it to him. I know it won't be easy for him to see me go through that, but if he realizes it only lasts a short time and I'm doing okay, I think it'll be better if he can talk with me. I'm going. End of discussion. Now, how about that tour?"

Emma knew there would be no convincing Travis otherwise, so she grabbed his arm and walked him through town.

"If you guys can't go to your homes, where does everyone sleep?"

"Most of us are at the hotel." Emma pointed.

"And the rest?"

Zeke interjected. "There are a few rooms above the grocery store and dress shop. The owners occupy them, and the blacksmith likes to sleep near the horses. He has a small area in the stables."

"What about a school? I don't see one." Travis squinted.

"It was just beyond the church."

Travis rubbed the back of his neck. "So it didn't make the cut?"

Zeke nodded.

As he walked inside each building, he felt like he had been visiting one of those ghost towns you hear about. They have the cowboy shooting shows twice a day and the rest of the time you're purchasing little trinkets. This time, however, they were real.

Inside the post office, the mail slots were still filled with letters to be delivered. The town left them there as a reminder of their past life. A chill feathered its way up his spine, and he shivered

When they got to the church at the edge of town, the light faded. Beyond it, there was nothing but blackness. He stood, mesmerized. The town was like an island floating in the middle of the dark sea.

There were no signs of life and the air grew so thick you could almost slice it with a blade. He put his foot out to try and go further, but whatever held them in the town clearly didn't want anyone crossing the line. When he tried to put his hand into the darkness, it wouldn't go past the edge of light. Like coming upon a brick wall under the cloak of a moonless night, the barrier was impenetrable.

Noah better figure out a way to break this curse, he thought. Less than two weeks to New Year's Day.

On the way back to the center of town, Travis stopped to gaze at the steeple. His site was drawn to the large brass bell.

"Do you ever ring that thing?" he pointed.

"It hasn't made a sound since we were banished here." Emma frowned.

"Is it okay to go inside?" Travis took a few steps toward the door.

"Of course. I come here often. Over the years it's helped me to cope with our fate."

Travis ambled to the door and before going inside, he bent over and brushed a powder of dirt from the leg of his pants. He then stomped his feet on the ground a few times before reaching for the iron handle. The door was lighter than he'd expected and swung open with ease. He stepped over the threshold and pulled the door shut. Emma and Zeke waited for him outside.

It was nothing like the churches he grew up visiting on Sunday mornings with his parents. There was no stained glass or elaborate statues of the saints. Marble and brass had been replaced by the modest design of ash and oak. Taking a seat in one of the several bare chairs, he gazed at the altar. A plain table draped in a white linen cloth was the center of this place of worship.

The simplicity of the space brought a calm to his nerves and he sighed.

Exiting the building, Travis found Emma and Zeke sitting on a nearby bench. He joined them and they headed back toward the center of town.

It would be a full twenty-four hours before they could walk through the gateway and see Noah, and Emma thought it best if Travis had some food and rested. It was going to be a rough trip.

145

Noah stood with his shoulders slouched, gazing at the empty doorway. Sirens were blaring in the distance and getting closer. Someone must have called them when they heard the gunshots. The Volgeling had gotten to their feet and were long gone. But Noah couldn't move. Even when Jon grabbed him by the arm and pulled, he couldn't.

"Noah! We have to go before the police get here. If we stay, then we'll jeopardize our chances of ever getting Travis and breaking the curse. We have to leave now. Come on."

Noah rubbed the back of his neck and stood up. Jon was right. They couldn't risk getting questioned by the police, or worse—detained. The two men ran around the block and then slowed down so they wouldn't draw any unwanted attention. Once they were in a safe distance they halted and sat down on the curb.

"We'll get him back. Just don't fall apart on me now. I need you to stay focused. Travis, Emma, Ezekiel, they're all depending on us to kill this bastard demon and break the curse. You need to be strong." Jon patted Noah's back.

"I'm okay. Just lost it for a second but I'm here now. But you...I saw you fall to the ground after we heard the shots. I thought you were dead."

"No, I just got punched in the gut and it knocked the wind out of me. My stomach is still sore."

"Hey, what was that name you called out when Emma was paralyzed? I could be wrong, but it looked like it freed her."

"It did. I was gonna tell you and Travis after our meeting tonight. I wasn't sure if was truth or just a guess my grandfather made, but according to an entry I found, it's the name of the demon."

"What the fuck? Why didn't you tell us at your office?" Noah clenched his fists at his side.

"Like I said, I wasn't sure and I didn't want to risk you mentioning it to Emma by mistake. If she brought that news back to everyone and it wasn't true...let's just say they don't need any more bad news. I thought later this evening we could flip through a few more pages of the journal to see if there was any evidence it was real."

"But when Emma got stuck..."

"I didn't think, just shouted."

"I'm glad you did. It worked."

"Now that we know the demon's name, let's see what we can find out about the former person."

"First, I think we should call someone to pick us up. We can't wait all night for the police to leave so we can go back and get the cars."

"You're right. But I don't want to have to answer questions. If I call my wife for a ride, then that will be another problem and I think we have our quota for problems filled right now."

"Agreed. There is someone I think I can call. She will wonder why the hell we're out here, but I know she won't ask any questions. I'll tell her the car broke down. You're a family friend and we were just running up to the bar for a drink. I think she'll be satisfied with that."

"Sounds good."

Noah pulled his cell phone out of his front pocket and dialed. "Hello, Jen?"

Chapter Thirteen

The slow drizzle of rain added to the misery of everything that had gone wrong that night and the temperature of thirty-seven degrees capped it off. Jen had been closing up at work when Noah called, so they had to wait about half an hour before she could get to them. Noah wasn't much for words and Jon seemed to be okay with it.

When Jen arrived, Noah stumbled into the car. The lie he was about to perpetrate on his friend was lathering on a thick layer of guilt.

"You okay?" Jen asked.

"Yeah, I'm fine. Just tired. Thanks so much for coming to get us. I didn't know who else to call. My mom and dad are at my aunt's and I didn't want to worry them."

"Sure, no problem. Just consider it payback for the rides to work." Jen looked around. "Hey, where's your car?"

"What?"

"Your car. You broke down. Where's your car?"

"Oh. We thought we'd start walking but it got too cold. It's up the street a bit. We'll get it in the morning."

"What were you doing up this way? Coming back from Travis's house?"

"Uh, yeah. We were going to the bar for a drink. Travis has some family in town, and they were doing the Strip thing." Noah sighed to himself. This lie was getting bigger by the second.

"Oh, cool. Did he say anything else about me?"

"Who?"

"Travis."

"Oh. No. Why, should he have?"

"Ugh. Never mind."

Noah kept quiet. He knew exactly what Jen was getting at, but how do you tell someone that the person they're interested in is worlds away? Literally.

Noah asked Jen to drop them off at his house. A logical request and one she'd expect. Afterward, he could borrow his dad's car to take Jon home. When they pulled up in front of the house, Jon got out first and made a call to his wife.

"Your friend seems nice," Jen said when they were alone.

"He is. Hey, thanks so much for coming out here to get us. We were freezing our asses off. Any longer and I think they would have found our frozen bodies on the sidewalk in the morning."

Jen grinned. "No problem. But when you have time, maybe sometime during the week, can we talk? I'd like to ask you something before New Year's Eve, okay?"

"I got a sec now. What's up?" Noah knew he really didn't have much time, but he didn't want to just brush Jen off. She was too nice and too good of a friend.

"I've been invited to a New Year's Eve party. One of my friends from church is having sort of an open house. I'd like to go, but I'd rather not go alone. I was wondering, do you think Travis would go with me if I asked him? I know he barely knows me, but maybe it could be fun. What do you think? You know him better than anyone, do you think he'd go?"

"You know, I think he mentioned his family was going out of town for New Year's. But I'll find out and let you know." Noah averted his eyes to the dimming streetlamp two houses down.

151

Jen frowned. "Okay. Thanks."

He felt like a creep and hated seeing that look on her face, but for now, it was the best solution. He had no idea where his friend was going to be on New Year's Eve. The thought made him sick to his stomach.

He gave her a hug and got out of the car. After she pulled away, he ran inside to get his dad's car keys. When he returned, Jon was just wrapping up his call to his wife.

"Okay, I'm sure she believed me. I told her I got a flat and I was having a truck come out and repair it. I really hate lying to her. I was thinking we could go grab a cup of coffee and then maybe in about an hour or so you could drop me off at my car. Things should have quieted down by then. I don't think the police really had anything to investigate. All the Volgeling were running off before they even got there. I can pick you up in the morning and take you to get your car."

"Sounds good to me. I'd rather keep my parents completely out of the loop on this one."

Jon nodded in agreement. "The fewer people involved, the better."

"There's something I wanted to show you tonight before all this shit happened. My mom got a package in the mail.

Well not exactly my mom; it was addressed to Thomas Finley and also had c/o J. Moreno on it. It's really old. Anyway, when I opened it, there was a weird little statue and a necklace. I'll show you tomorrow. It's in the trunk of my car."

"That's strange. Why would it be addressed to me and go to your house? We didn't even know each other until a few days ago."

"Yeah, it's one for the strange and unusual. Also, Thomas Finley, the boy from the town who wandered off and didn't get snatched into the abyss, was the sender as well as the recipient. Emma is gonna be happy. He was Joseph's little brother and they never knew if he'd survived past that day. "

"Okay. Weird just catapulted to what the fuck?" Jon rolled his eyes.

It was a quick ride to the local IHOP, where pancakes always made everything seem better. Although Noah doubted they'd have their same appeal tonight. After being seated and served their coffee, Noah asked the question that had been bubbling its way to his voice.

"Jon, what was that wooden statue you used on Emma to free her? It was similar to the one I found in the box."

"It belonged to my great-grandfather. It has been passed down to each generation, but up until tonight, I didn't realize its strength. Truthfully, I thought it was more of a good luck charm. Not symbolic on either side of my family history but something my great-grandfather was given by a settler from the other side of the valley for protection. I guess the guy liked him and they had a limited friendship."

"That's a weird way to describe friends." Noah sipped his coffee.

"Yeah, back then the settlers from Utah didn't co-mingle with other groups. That's why when James and Dallen fell in love it caused such upheaval. Marrying out of your kind was prohibited. Hell, back then the Utah settlers would arrange the marriages and neither the daughters nor the sons had a choice. Dallen broke tradition simply by following her heart."

Noah clenched his fist on the table. "All of this for something so stupid. Love is love. No one can make you love someone. You do or you don't."

"The world is full of ignorance and misunderstanding."

"Well, I'm just glad you shouted out the bastard's name. If you hadn't freed Emma, she'd be dead now."

154

"Yeah. I know. My father told me to always have it with me, and now I know why. I wasn't sure if anything would happen, but I thought it was worth a shot. That thing had a strong hold on her, and it threw you around like you were a piece of paper. Lucky it worked."

"We have to go up on the mountain and get that damn blade. I think it's going to be the only way to get Travis back and save the town...and you. But first, we really need to find out how to locate this fucking demon. We can't just wait for it to appear. There must be some way to summon it so when we do find the hatchet we'll be ready to use it."

"Agreed. We still have some journals of my grandfather's that we haven't gone through yet. Maybe they could tell us what we need to know. After I pick you up in the morning, we'll go straight to my office."

"Okay. First thing in the morning then. Say seven?"

"Seven o'clock is good. I think we could probably go get my car now. It's getting late and I don't want my wife to start worrying or worse, asking questions."

When they reached the street where the cars were parked, it was quiet. You would have never guessed that just a short time ago it was the scene of total chaos. But still, something felt out of place. And although he couldn't quite figure out why, Noah had a chill of eeriness running up the center of his back. He felt like their every move was under surveillance and the shadow of the looming mountain just seemed to add to the uncomfortable weight of the air. Normally, he loved this mountain; it was a sanctuary to him. When he was having a bad day at work or his dad was undergoing some new medication, this mountain calmed him. But not tonight. No. Tonight it held fear. They were going to have to go up there and search for the hatchet. They would face several men trying to kill them and a demon who could wipe them out in a mere breath. His solace had been stolen from him.

"Jon, we can't forget to bring the map of Sunrise Mountain that shows the whereabouts of the hatchet."

"It's in the safe at the office."

"I'll do some more research tonight. Maybe I can come up with something, anything, that can help us."

The men parted ways and Noah flopped into the driver's seat. Gazing at the stencil of peaks in his rear-view mirror, his jaw stiffened.

Only four days until New Year's.

Chapter Fourteen

Jon picked Noah up at seven as planned. It had been a long night of staring at the ceiling and Noah was exhausted, so when he got into the car he just slouched down and closed his eyes. When they reached the coffee shop, Jon had to nudge him to wake up. "Hey, Noah. We're here. What the hell did you do last night?"

"Research."

"All night?"

"Yep. And I didn't find a damn thing that could help us."

"Well, let's get some coffee and grab a bite. We can go over what we've got. I swung by my office and grabbed the journals. I thought we could go over them while we were eating and get a head start on this."

"Good idea. I'm really getting scared. We have less than two weeks left and I got nothing. I know we need to find the hatchet, but if we can't call this thing out, all of it will be pointless.

Besides, I don't want to have to tell Travis's parents that, well... I don't know what the hell I'd tell his parents. Jon, he's my best friend. I mean I can't remember a time when we didn't hang out. I can't let him down."

"We'll figure this out. I have no choice. All I can think about is my unborn son. What legacy do I leave him if we fail? To know his life will end just as it's starting. And what if he has a son? I can't be responsible for this fate being left to any other male born in this family. This has to work. We'll find the hatchet and we will find the demon."

Noah dropped his chin and rubbed his forehead. He knew he needed to hold it together. The server came over to take their order and bring them coffee, and after a few minutes their breakfast arrived. In addition to the eggs, pancakes, and bacon they each ordered, the server set down two slices of pecan pie.

They both looked at each other. "Miss, I think you made a mistake with our order."

The woman looked at Jon with a perplexed expression. "No. You both ordered the pancake special and that's what I brought you. Did you want something different?"

"Yes, we did order the special, but we never asked for pie."

She chuckled. "Oh, I'm so sorry. That was sent over by your friend."

The two men straightened up. "Our friend? Where? Who?" Jon was gathering up the journals while Noah looked anxiously around the room.

"He's sitting right over...well that's odd. He was there just a second ago. A thin gentleman with dark hair and little gold-rimmed glasses. He was dressed in a gray suit and he was very nice. He asked me to get you each a piece of pie and put it on his bill. Is there a problem?"

Noah continued to scour the room but saw no sign of the guy she was describing.

"Uh, no. Could we get our check, please? We are kind of in a hurry."

"But you haven't touched your food."

"Please."

The woman frowned. "Uh…sure thing. I'll be right back." As the server went to tally the bill, Noah helped Jon gather the rest of the journals. Whoever that man was, he was playing with them, and they needed to get out of there immediately.

When she brought the check, they thanked her and quickly left. Jon drove Noah to his car and they agreed to meet at his office.

Before driving away, Noah cautiously grabbed the package from the trunk and set it beside him on the passenger seat. He reflected on the incident at Travis's when his knife grazed Thomas's name on the address. This time, he was careful not to make contact.

When they arrived at the office, Jon's receptionist was already there. He instructed her to not disturb him unless it was his wife calling and they shut the door. Jon sat down at his desk, and Noah across from him in the familiar chair from their first meeting. They spread the journals out and Noah placed the box in front of him. Jon picked it up.

"Interesting. The wood tells me it's extremely old. Maybe almost two-hundred years." He opened the lid.

"See, doesn't that statue resemble yours?"

"It does, but this one is different. See the instrument he's holding? It's a horn."

"Yeah, so?"

Jon pulled the wooden figure from his pocket. "Look, it's dressed in robes, but no horn."

"What does it mean?"

"I think it means that once we kill the demon with the hatchet, we can banish him into your statue.

161

The one you hold is molded from gold and the horn represents victory, which is what it'll be once it's confined. My talisman was created for protection, so no horn."

"But if the demon's banished back to hell, why do we need to do this?"

"To keep anyone from raising him again. It'll be his own private hell."

"How do you know this?"

"I've dealt with antiquities most of my adult life. I've traveled to many countries and have seen several versions of this deity. Different regions vary slightly but the intent seems to be similar. It's a prison. Jedediah Smith will be bound to the statue for eternity."

"I can live with that. And the necklace?"

Jon placed the statue back in the box and picked up the necklace. Studying the details of the pendant, he noticed a small inscription on the back.

"Did you see this?" Jon pointed to the writing.

"No. What is it?"

"It looks like maybe a name? It's so small, I nearly missed it. Hang on."

J

on got up from his desk and sauntered to a bookcase in the corner of the room and snatched something off the shelf. When he sat down he placed the object up to his right eye.

"Is that the same thing a jeweler uses?"

"Yes, an eye loupe. It comes in handy when trying to bargain with sellers who claim their object is authentic. This little tool reveals the truth."

"Which is?"

"They're trying to sell me a very good copy of the real thing."

"Damn."

"There's a name. It's Dallen. This necklace belonged to the girl that killed herself. Wait...I can barely make it out, but there's something else... Isaiah 40:29."

"What does that mean?"

"Hang on, I've seen this before."

Jon opened the middle drawer of his desk and pulled out a calendar. Setting it down on his desktop, he hurriedly flipped through each month.

"Here! He giveth power to the faint; and to them that have no might, he increase the strength."

"I don't get it." Noah raised a brow.

"It means that God gives power to the ones who need it the most. I think someone gave the necklace to Dallen to protect her."

"Yeah, well, it didn't work."

"Obviously."

"Without knowing who gave it to her I don't think it helps."

"I know, but it's all I got right now. But think about this. Thomas sent it a long time ago. Maybe he hoped we'd figure out how to use it. Maybe Dallen didn't know how to or didn't care. Her true love was dead."

"That's a lot of maybe's. Let's discuss something we can do something about. The dessert bandit from the restaurant."

"Whoever that guy is, he was just messing with us. Letting us know we're being watched. Maybe he thinks it'll scare us."

Noah looked up. "Well, I don't know about you, but it fucking scared me. But he's wrong if he thinks it'll make us quit."

"Let's get back to the books."

Several hours passed and neither one had found anything helpful. They decided to try the library one last time and see if they might have missed something—anything, about the demon.

Noah swiped his palms along the sides of his jeans. They only had a few hours before dusk. He had to have something to tell Travis. He knew he must be freaking out by now and not having any news would just make it worse. If he could at least give him an ounce of hope to hold onto then maybe he could keep him stable until they got him back. He was scouring a paragraph on the supernatural's relation to the original Utah settlers, when he spotted it.

There was a remaining portion of the chapter that spoke specifically about Jedediah Smith. Most of the contents contained information about the demon they already knew, but further down the page, Noah caught a word...summon. There it was. The ritual to summon the demon at will. When recited, Jedediah must come. As he was reading, the blood pumped through his veins like cars at a back alley drag race. He grinned. It was something to tell Travis.

He turned the book around to show Jon, who was immersed in his reading, but before he could get a word out he clutched his belly. A tsunami of queasiness splashed in his gut and his palms were dripping with sweat. He tried to get up, but the room began to spin.

He nearly fell off the chair but clutched the table in time to anchor himself to the seat.

"Noah." Jon ran to his side. "What's wrong? Are you okay?"

"I feel really dizzy and nauseous. I don't know, it just came over me all of a sudden. What the hell is that smell?"

Jon looked up and scoured the room. He remembered what Travis had said about the awful smell every time the demon was close. "Noah, get up."

"I don't think I can. I feel really sick. Besides, I found it. I know what we need to do to summon the demon."

"Noah, listen to me. You have to get up. We have to get out of here. Now."

"But Jon. You're not listening to me. I found..." But before Noah could finish his sentence Jon pulled him up, grabbed the book, and headed for the door.

"Noah, I don't want to scare you, but something's pulling me back."

Jon pushed forward, trudging one leg in front of the other as if he'd fallen into a freshly laid foundation of cement.

"Jedediah Smith!" he shouted.

Breaking free from the demon's grasp, they approached the first exit, but the door slammed shut. Noah's eyes widened as he bolted for another way out. Nothing like a demon to make you forget about the vomit stuck in the back of your throat.

"Noah. Go for the door on the west side of the building." As the two men tried to escape, books flew off the shelves, laying a maze of destruction in their path. The once quiet crowd of readers released ear-piercing shrills and ran for safety, pushing them further away from freedom. Jon took the totem from his pocket and began chanting the same words he used to help Emma the night before. A pathway cleared in front of them, leading directly to the exit. They made a swift dash for the doors, slammed into them and stumbled outside. Keeping the momentum, they raced for the car and drove to Jon's office.

Jon opted to park in the underground garage and use the service elevator to his office. When they were inside the building, he took out the totem and created a circular motion in front of the office door. "I call to the spirits who have gone before me. Blood to blood, past to present. Protect this office and all its occupants from harm, letting no unwanted beings cross this path."

"What did you just do?"

"I put a protection spell on the office. Let's just hope it's strong enough to keep the demon out."

"And you thought it was just a good luck charm." Noah gave him a smirk.

"Yeah, well, just be happy I listened when my father taught me this stuff. Even if I thought it was all just stories. Now let's see what you found."

"Here at the bottom of the page, the last paragraph. It states step by step what we have to do. Everything must be specific to the instructions and there's a list of everything we'll need." Noah turned the page. "Wait. This can't be right."

"What is it? Is something wrong?"

"Uh, yeah. It must be missing some pages. Look. This paragraph is about something totally different. It goes from page 101 to page 104. Two pages are missing. Crap. Without that list and the rest of the instructions, this damn book is useless."

Jon grabbed it and leafed through it.

"Jon, you can fucking look at that thing all day. It's not going to make the pages magically appear. We need to get the hell out of here and go back to the library. Maybe we can find something else."

"No. It isn't safe."

"We have no choice. I can't think of anything else. Can you?" Noah's questions were drenched in sarcasm. He was losing patience and Jon's reaction to all of this was really pissing him off.

"Actually, I can. This book looks very familiar to me."

Noah rolled his eyes. Running his fingers through his hair he grabbed a chunk and took a deep breath.

"Every book we've gone through the past few days looks relatively the same. Of course, it's going to look familiar to you. But this is the first time I picked it up. I promise you, I've never seen it before and neither have you."

Jon just shook his head again. "That's where you're wrong. Yes. You probably haven't seen it before, but I have. This book, one just like it, is at my aunt's house in Utah. I know it. There were several books still in the attic. There were too many for me to carry back on the plane so I grabbed the ones that seemed like they might contain information that was useful to us. This book is primarily about factual events. I had no idea it contained any folklore or stories about Jedediah. I missed that when I was scouring through it. We have to go to Utah."

Chapter Fifteen

Jon sat with his feet propped up on his desk. His head lay back on his chair and his eyes were closed. He'd booked the first flight out for the both of them.

"I hate waiting," Noah sighed.

"Yeah, me too kid. But at least we got a flight.

Noah sat gazing out the window until the sudden ring from his phone tickled his spine.

"Hey. Jen? What's up? Oh crap. Yeah, I'm coming. I just got tied up with my dad. I'll be there in a few minutes."

Noah got off the phone and grabbed the car keys. "Look, Jon, I gotta run over to work. I forgot my shift, I should have been there a half an hour ago. I'll stay long enough to find a way to get out of there. I'll meet you at the church at dusk, can you get a ride?"

"Sure. Go. I'll get a cab. I booked us a flight for eight o'clock tonight. We can go to the airport after we see Travis and the others. And Noah, be on guard."

"I will. See you there. And Jon, you be careful, too."

When Noah reached the store it was empty, not a customer in sight. Greg, the assistant manager had stepped away for a few minutes on his break and Jen was standing at the counter folding t-shirts. She glared at him as he approached her.

"I know, I know. Don't look at me like that. My dad was having trouble, so I'm late, so sue me."

"Wow. I never thought I'd see the day." Jen looked pissed.

"What? You're going to tell me this place is more important than my dad?"

"No. I never thought I'd see the day that you actually lied to me right to my face. Noah, I stopped over at your house. Greg called when I was on my way to work. He said he had tried your cell because you were already fifteen minutes late. I saw your dad, you weren't there, and he hadn't seen you. He figured you left early for work, only you weren't at work. Where were you? Why do you feel you need to lie to me? Are you in some sort of trouble? I can help. I thought you trusted me. I thought we were friends."

Noah stared at her, struggling to find the right words to ease the tension. If he told her the truth she'd never believe him, and he would risk exposing her to unforeseen danger.

On the other hand, if he kept lying it would just keep growing until it blew up in his face worse than the confrontation they were having. He thought for a second and realized it didn't matter if it blew up in his face. Her safety outweighed any confrontation they might have, even if it meant their friendship. No. He had to keep lying to Jen. It was the only choice he had.

"I uh...met someone."

"What? You met someone? Who? When?"

"She's not from around here. We met last week when I was working. She had come into the store on your day off. We sort of clicked and started going out. I'm not sure if she's staying, so I didn't introduce her to anyone yet. I wanted to wait and see how things go. Anyway, that's who I've been with and why I was late today. Satisfied? I'm sorry I lied. I should have trusted you."

Jen turned away and gazed out of the store window.

"Jen? You okay?"

"I'm fine. Just not sure if I believe you."

Noah gulped. Jen never questioned him before. She was really hurt, and he didn't know how to fix this. But right now, he didn't have the time.

He had to leave and get over to the church before dusk ended. For now he'll just have to let her be angry with him.

"Look, Jen, I'm sorry if you don't believe me. That's the truth and I don't know what else to tell you. I have to go, though. Do you think you can cover for me? Maybe tell Greg I was puking my guts out or something?"

Jen rolled her eyes. "Are you freaking kidding me? First, you lie to me, then you tell me what I think is another lie on top of that, and now you're asking me to cover for you? You're unbelievable. I don't know what's really going on with you, Noah, but you're blowing it. Get the hell out of here. I'm not doing this to cover for you. I'm doing it because I can't stand to look at you right now. Call me when you're ready to tell me the real truth."

Noah felt like crap. He wanted to sit down and tell her everything, but he couldn't.

He just murmured thank you under his breath and left. He would have to really work to fix this after everything was over. Hopefully, Travis would be there to help him explain. And Emma.

Noah arrived at the church a few minutes before dusk. Jon was already there and holding a small bag. He was sitting on one of the decorative landscape rocks.

Noah moped over and sat next to him.

"Something happen?"

"It's Jen. She found out I was lying to her and now she doesn't even want to be in the same room with me. I've known her for so long. I'd hate to lose her as a friend, but right now I don't have a choice."

"One problem at a time."

"Yeah. I know."

"You'll get your chance to explain later."

"I sure hope so. What's in the bag?"

Jon opened the bag and pulled out a small revolver. "I thought we could use this."

"Are you nuts? They won't let you on the plane with that thing." Noah's eyes widened.

"I'm going to check my bag. I do have a concealed weapons permit for Nevada, Utah, and Arizona. The way I travel, with all the high-dollar items I purchase, it's just some extra security. I figured we could use some of that extra security right about now."

Noah looked up at the church. He heard the humming sound. "They're coming."

As they stepped onto the small cement slab in front of the archway, Ezekiel and Emma were holding up Travis.

"Ezekiel, can you hold Travis on your own?" asked Emma.

"Sure."

Emma ran to meet Noah before he could reach his friend. She grabbed his hand and pulled him aside.

"Emma, what's wrong with him? Is he okay?" Noah turned back to Travis. "Emma, tell me."

"Travis is fine. He is just feeling what we all do in the beginning when passing through. It will get easier for him the more he journeys. It takes a few minutes to feel strong again. We urged him to stay back, but he wouldn't listen."

Ezekiel helped Travis to the ground and walked over to Noah and Emma.

"I am going for supplies, Emma. We still need to feed everyone. " Emma went to follow him. "No. You stay and help with Travis."

"No brother, let's give them time to talk. I think Travis will be fine."

Travis nodded in agreement.

Noah glanced over at Jon. "Maybe you should go with him and take your security with you. We don't know where that thing or the Volgeling are and the last attack on them was at the school."

"Good idea. We'll be back shortly."

Noah immediately went to Travis. He sat down and gave him a pat on the back. Travis looked up and Noah held his breath. His friend looked as white as chalk. There were dark circles under his eyes, and he was sweating and shivering at the same time. Travis flashed a smile to let him know he was okay.

"I know it looks bad, but I'm okay. Really. It will pass soon."

"When? Just in time for you to go back?"

"Dude. Stop with the drama. I'm fine. You have more important things going on right now. Like maybe rescuing my sorry ass. Okay?" Travis shoved him in the shoulder.

"If you say so." Noah raised a brow. "We have a lead that we need to follow up on. It's a book that contains a summoning spell. We can use it after we find the hatchet. We're going to Utah tonight to get it from Jon's aunt's house. We'll come back tomorrow afternoon and I'll be here tomorrow night to let you know everything. But you don't have to come through. I can tell Emma."

"Dude. Enough. I'll see you tomorrow night. Everything else okay?"

"We had another run-in with the demon, but we're here, so yeah, everything's okay. What's it like over there?"

"It's so bright. I wish I could have told you to bring me some shades. And nothing moves. I mean not even a blade of grass. There's no breeze, it's like the air is stagnant or something, and it's sort of cold. Which is weird because of how bright it is. You'd think it'd be scorching, but it isn't. I don't know how they made it this long. I'd have lost it for sure. If we get stuck permanently, dying will be a relief."

"Shut the fuck up! Trav, I'll get you all back. I will."

Travis forced a half-smile and stood up.

"Hey, I showed Jon the statue and the necklace. They're not just random artifacts, there's a meaning attached to them."

"Oh yeah, what?"

"The statue... "

Ezekiel approached with Emma beside him, and she reached out and tugged on Travis's arm.

"I guess our conversation's over." Travis tried to steady himself.

"Trav. Don't forget, you're coming home."

"Travis, we must go." Emma tugged at his arm.

Noah's jaw tightened.

"You okay, Dude?" asked Travis.

"Uh. Yeah." Noah brushed a strand of hair from Emma's cheek. "I'll see you tomorrow."

Her pinky finger gently glided over his, clinging to him for one more second before parting.

As they were stepping through the doorway, Noah shouted, "Trav!"

"Yeah?"

"Hang in there."

He flashed a smile. "You know me. A little vacay, some sun. I'll be good."

Jon and Noah got to the airport about an hour before their flight was going to take off, so they headed to the bar for a drink. Noah couldn't get his conversation with Travis out of his head. Three days left until the curse would take his best friend, and the girl he loved. Even though Travis tried to put on a good show for him, he knew he was already getting affected by the abyss. His best friend was the joker; always seeming like things just rolled off of him. But Noah knew better. He was friends with him too long to be fooled with humor or a fake smile. His friend was scared. Whatever it felt like on the other side, Travis preferred death. Not a good sign.

The two men stared at the Raiders vs. Steelers game on the flat screen, and when the flight was announced they headed over to boarding. While they were waiting in line, Noah noticed a tall man carrying a brown leather satchel. He was neatly dressed in dark blue jeans, a gray V-neck sweater, and a distressed charcoal leather jacket. His tennis shoes glistened like they had just been taken out of the box and a plain silver cross hung an inch below his collarbone. His short, black hair and perfectly trimmed beard looked more runway model than business class. He kept to himself and didn't even look up at the attendant checking tickets as they boarded.

He wasn't sure why this man stood out to him, but Noah watched his every move. When they were seated he leaned into Jon and pointed out the stranger. Jon didn't recognize him and shrugged it off as paranoia, but Noah couldn't let go of the uneasy feeling. He decided to keep an inconspicuous eye on him for the rest of the flight.

After they were airborne, the flight attendant came by offering sodas and other drinks while handing out small bags of pretzels. Noah wasn't hungry but he opened the bag and started munching on the snack for something to do. He kept glancing over at his new focus for the next ninety minutes trying to figure out why this man drew him in.

The stranger was gazing out the window and never moved from his seat. Halfway through the flight, Noah decided that his new mission wasn't going anywhere at thirty-five thousand feet. He lay his head back and closed his eyes.

He saw Emma. She was walking along Charleston Boulevard with a picturesque Sunrise Mountain behind her. The air was crisp, a contrast to the golden rays caressing her face. She was smiling as she walked toward him. Travis and Ezekiel were a few paces behind her, and they were laughing at Henry, who was running through an empty lot chasing a pigeon that kept landing and taking flight.

They were happy. He couldn't wait to take her in his arms. She was so beautiful. The sunlight danced across her long locks, highlighting streaks of honey and gold. He was never able to see the brilliance in the cloak of dusk.

But as she approached, a cold shiver ran down his back. Clouds rushed to cover the sun, and darkness ushered in fear. Henry collapsed in the field and turned to dust. Then Ezekiel and Travis. A roaring gale suddenly surrounded him, taking the remains of his friends. Emma screamed for him and he tried to run to her, but an unseen force held him in place. The familiar foul scent permeated through the air, burning his nostrils. He was powerless as his love crumbled and scattered with the wind.

"Noah. Hey, wake up, we're landing," Jon whispered.

Gasping, he quickly opened his eyes. The horror of his dream frightened him into breathlessness. As he struggled to regain composure, the flight attendant moved down the aisle, motioning for them to buckle up as the plane descended. He closed his eyes once again, and for the first time since he was a kid, pleaded to the universe for help.

Chapter Sixteen

They hailed a cab to take them to Jon's aunt's house. On the way, Noah thought he saw the tall man from the flight driving past them two lanes over. A chill snaked its way up his spine as he tried to follow the car with his gaze, losing it as the vehicle weaved through traffic and sped off.

It was nearly eleven o'clock when they pulled up to the remote destination of Timber Lakes. The ominous two-story home was completely dark as they drove through the oversized black wrought iron gates. Noah felt like he was in an episode of *Stranger Things*. Any minute they'd cross the realm into the Upside Down and the Demogorgon would be waiting to shred them into pieces.

Hell, who was he kidding? They were already stuck in the Upside Down. Except the Demogorgon had been replaced with a vengeful demon.

The taxi let them out in front and Jon pulled a key from his pocket and opened the door. When they got inside, Noah briskly rubbed his arms. Jon flipped on the wall switch and a table lamp illuminated the room.

"Wait here, I'll turn on some more lights," said Jon.

Noah scanned the room while he waited. Overstuffed brown leather chairs and a sofa with heavy tapestry fabric faced the fireplace. Peering through the archway, he found a large circular foyer dressed in doors.

Jon came back into the room and motioned for Noah to sit down while he built a fire. When an orange and red glow danced across the hearth, Jon went into the kitchen and made some coffee. Noah couldn't help it, but he kept having the feeling like they were being watched. He got up and went to a large window that overlooked the back of the house. He parted the drapes and squinted. An in-ground pool and what looked like a guest house were at the far end of the property.

That's it. Nothing lurking about or standing ready with claws bared to turn them into its next meal. Breathing a sigh of relief, he went over to warm himself by the fire. Jon brought the coffee in and placed it on the table.

"You feeling warmer?"

"Yeah. I'm okay."

"Then we better get started in the attic. The sooner we find the book and the instructions, the sooner we can get back home."

Noah nodded in agreement.

Jon led him to a large mahogany door at the end of the hallway on the second floor. Walking up the steps, Noah glided his hand across the glassy shine of the thick banister until they abruptly stopped.

"How many doors are in this place?" Noah raised a brow.

"Too many to count."

Peering over Jon's shoulder, Noah's jaw dropped when he opened the door.

The room was not the dust-drenched attic he was expecting. Living in Vegas, he had never been in an attic. He only knew what he had seen in movies or television. Dark, unfinished, and creepy. This was the complete opposite. A huge brass bed with an upright mahogany dresser and mirror were placed in the center of the elegantly decorated room. On each side of the bed, round end tables served as pedestals for two Victorian vintage lamps. The comforter was a pale green with tiny pink roses and ruffled shams. An olive velvet couch was across the room complete with a cherry-wood coffee table and a stand-up antique brass lamp. A large roll-top desk called out to anyone who wished to write a letter.

This is something Emma might have seen in her day, he thought to himself.

Jon ambled to another table that was hidden in the corner of the room by the couch. An assortment of books piled neatly in three stacks lined the cherry-top finish. He carefully pulled a leather-bound volume from the middle of the lowest pile.

"Here it is. I knew it."

While Jon was leafing through the book looking for the pages that had been missing from the copy in the library, Noah picked up another one and began reading. Sitting on the edge of the brass bed, he became engrossed in the words. After a few minutes, he stood up. He was completely stunned by what he had read and made his way over to Jon, holding his place in the book.

"Jon. Listen to this, it's amazing. Apparently, the Volgeling aren't the only ones out there. There's a chapter in here about a group that calls themselves the Order of Protectors. But they're not trying to help the demon. Just the opposite. They're here to protect the one who is meant to break the curse."

"The one who will break the curse? What does that mean?"

"I'm not sure, but I think there's somebody who is chosen. You know, the whole *the force is strong with this one* thing."

"What?"

"Dude. It's a Star Wars reference. You know, Luke...Darth Vader...Star Wars."

Jon shook his head. " Oh, yeah. I've never seen it."

"You've never seen Star Wars? Not one of them?"

"Nope. I'm less sci-fi and more sports. Like *Rudy*, that's a great movie. Or *The Way Back*, that's an awesome film."

"Shit. When this is over we need to get you educated. Sports is okay but Star Wars is supreme."

Jon rolled his eyes. "Enough Star Wars. Here they are, the missing pages."

As he read through the ritual for summoning the demon, Noah flipped through the remaining chapter of the book. He froze suddenly. The buzzing in his head was deafening.

It couldn't be. It wasn't, and yet... "Jon. You need to look at this."

"I'm trying to finish. What is it?"

"Look at this picture. Anybody you know?"

Jon studied the face. The man was wearing a World War II Army uniform.

"What? No... wait. It sort of looks like that guy on the plane."

"Yeah. I told you that dude was creepy."

"I said *sort of* looks like him. Noah, we're letting our imaginations get the best of us. If it is him, he'd be about ninety right now."

"No. Look. That's him. I know it. It says here his name is Arthur Markham."

"Who is...*was* he?"

Noah knitted his brow. "After everything we've experienced, everything *your family* has experienced, you're really going to question whether or not this is the same guy? It says he was a captain and rescued a bunch of prisoners from the Germans. He's the one who started the Order of Protectors. He's like the head honcho. I don't know how, but I do know this is the same guy. But I think I was wrong about him being out to get us. If he's here, it must be because he's watching over the chosen guy."

"Noah..."

"Shh. You hear that?" Noah grabbed Jon's arm and motioned for him to whisper.

"I didn't hear..." There was a creaking from the floor below them. "Yeah. I heard that."

"Someone's in the house with us."

Cautiously, the two men got up and stepped heel to toe to the stairs.

Noah whispered, "I think we should…"

A man's arm, exposing the symbol of a partially blocked Sun on the palm of his hand, reached out suddenly and grabbed hold of Jon, yanking him halfway down the staircase.

"Noah!"

Noah reached out for Jon, but the only thing he clutched was air.

He tried to follow him, but someone latched onto his shirt and pulled him back up. The door slammed shut as he pivoted around to see who it was. His eyes widened when he recognized the tall stranger from the plane. And standing beside him was….

"Jen? What the fuck? What the hell are you doing here? And why are you with this guy? What's going on?"

"Noah, listen. I know you're confused but let's get out of here and I promise you, we'll explain everything." Jen grabbed his arm and pulled him toward the window.

"No! I'm not leaving without Jon. We have to go back and get him. Those sons of bitches down there are killers. We can't leave him."

"I understand that you're concerned about the safety of your friend. But they won't kill him. They'll use him as a bargaining tool to get what they want, so he is safe for now," said the stranger from the plane.

"What do you mean get what they want? What the hell do they want?"

"You. Noah, they want you. If you want to help your friend and the others, please, give us a chance."

"Dude, are you on crack? Why the hell would they want me?"

"Arthur, we don't have time for this. We have to get him out of here now. They're gonna be coming through that door any second." Jen pursed her lips.

"Noah, you're going to have to trust us. Look, you know Jen. She wouldn't lie to you."

"You're kidding me, right? Dude you really gonna stand there and play that card?" Noah's voice cracked with sarcasm. She wouldn't lie? Who the hell *was* she? He didn't know anything anymore and he sure wasn't going to believe what she said at this point. "I don't know what the hell is going on. And even though I think we might be on the same side, I don't trust you. And I'm not leaving my friend."

"Arthur. They're coming through!" They could hear a pounding on the door and the whump of metal breaking through the wood.

"I'm sorry, we don't have any more time for this."

The stranger took something out of his pocket and Noah stepped back. Jen grabbed him from behind and squeezed him tight so he couldn't move. Startled, Noah whipped around and overpowered her, throwing Jen to the ground. He felt a pinch in his neck and a warm river shimmied through his veins as his legs wobbled beneath him. He dropped to his knees and struggled to focus through the fuzzy haze.

He looked up at Jen, who had managed to get back on her feet. "What did you...." Noah lost consciousness.

Noah stirred. A dialogue of low-pitched voices surrounded him, and he slowly opened his eyes. His muscles tensed when he remembered what had happened. Reaching for the top of his head, he winced. The drummer in his brain was playing a solo at his expense.

Slowly turning his head, a queen-sized bed took up residence in the room about four feet away.

Traveling his gaze from the gaudy maroon and gold comforter that covered whatever secrets lie below on the mattress, he noticed the same cheap covering laying across his legs.

He rolled over to his side and tried to stand, but he was still woozy and fell to the floor. Two arms clasped around his waist and eased him up, keeping a tight grip as they helped him to a two-cushioned couch.

He looked up and saw Jen.

"Where the hell are we? How long was I out?"

"We're at a motel in Vegas, and you were asleep about seven or eight hours," she said calmly.

"How did we get here?"

"Arthur drove us. We couldn't take you back by plane, that would've been too hard to explain."

"What the fuck, Jen?"

"Here, I brought you some water." She reached over to a glass that was on the table beside the couch. "Drink it slow. Are you feeling sick to your stomach at all?" She sounded concerned.

Noah wasn't buying it. She was a part of this, and he no longer trusted her. "What the hell do you care?"

"Noah. No matter what you might think, I'm still your friend. That hasn't changed. I know there's a lot we need to talk about, but first I wanna make sure you're okay."

"You drug me and now you're worried about me? A bit of a cliché, don't you think?"

"Here, take this." Jen handed him a little pink tablet.

"What? The job was incomplete and now you want to finish it?"

"It's Pepto, you idiot. Just chew it. You'll feel better."

She sounded just like the Jen he knew. But she wasn't, and that killed him. That Jen was always there for him or anyone who needed her. But this person...he was so confused.

"In a few minutes, you'll feel better and we'll talk. Arthur will be back by then and I promise you, we'll explain everything. Rest for now, though. You're gonna need it."

Noah laid his head on the back of the couch and closed his eyes. All he could think about was Jon. He felt helpless. Jon was with killers, Travis was trapped in the abyss and Emma and the entire town were facing their demise.

Things were hard enough when his dad had been diagnosed with prostate cancer, but at least there were doctors and treatments. His dad had a good chance at getting better, even if the journey was difficult. Going against this demon and the curse, no treatment or doctor could save them. If they failed, he would lose just about everyone he loved, and Jon would leave a continuing legacy of fear and death. Too much was going on in his head as he slowly got back up again.

Jen ran over. "Noah, it's too soon. You need more time to rest."

"Yeah, well, that's the one thing I don't have. Now please just get out of my way."

"Jen. Let him go."

Noah heard that same voice from the attic. The tall man was back. "We're not holding you prisoner. You're free to leave whenever you want, but don't you want to know who we are?"

"I know who you are. You're the Order of the Protectors. Right?"

"Ah, you've been reading."

"I've been reading." Noah's sarcasm dripped off his words like a thick syrup falling on a plate of pancakes. He wanted them to know his discontent.

"What I don't know is how you're standing there looking as young as my father when you should be what? Over a hundred. Right? Tell me, how is it you're still so young? No. Wait. I know. You're cursed too. Have I got it?"

"Noah." Jen furrowed her brow. "How about you give us five minutes to explain before running your mouth off and acting like a horse's ass?"

"Fine. Explain then. Tell me everything like you promised." He sat down on the edge of the couch and nervously cracked his knuckles.

Jen sat down next to him and the stranger grabbed a chair from the table in the adjoining room. He also grabbed the books that Noah and Jon had found at the house and placed them on the table beside the couch. Noah immediately grabbed both of them and clutched them close to his chest. They were not leaving his possession. They were the only key to saving everyone.

"Let me properly introduce myself. My name is Arthur Markham."

He put his hand out to shake, but Noah just pulled back further. He didn't trust this man yet and he wasn't shaking his hand. For all he knew, he had his own agenda. After all, why else would he be here? And what the hell did he want from him?

"Okay. I understand. You don't trust me yet. But I hope after you hear what I have to say you'll have a little more faith in me and us."

"Whatever, we're running out of time, so can you just get to it?"

"Yes. You're right. Back in nineteen thirty-nine, I was serving my country as a captain in the army. I was never one for family and thought the service would be a good career for me. When the war broke out, I was sent to Europe. There I met a younger man, Charles was his name. He told me a story. We had both been out on leave and drinking. He was extremely troubled as were all of us. What was happening to innocent people there would turn any man's stomach, but his was more than that. He had a secret. One that was eating away his insides. He told me about this town and Nevada and his family curse."

"His family?"

"Yes. This man, Charles, was Jon Moreno's grandfather. He was tortured by his family's fate and the people of the banished town, but he had been unsuccessful in finding the answers he needed to break the curse."

"Wait. You believed him? The both of you were drinking. You said so yourself. What the hell made you think his story was true?"

"I believed him because I could see the truth in his eyes. They were filled with so much pain and despair. I know it sounds crazy, but I believed every word. We became very close friends during that time. We watched out for each other and got through the war. When it was over I decided to go back with him to Nevada and help. I had no family of my own as I told you, so there was nothing stopping me. We almost cracked the curse a few times, but the Volgeling always seemed to be one step ahead of us."

"Okay, but that doesn't explain you... how you look. And Jen. How do you know him?"

"He's my great-grandfather."

Noah's eyes widened at Arthur. "Wait. You said you didn't have any family."

"I hadn't. But when I went to Nevada the unexpected happened and I met a lovely woman. We married and had a daughter, Jen's grandmother." Arthur turned away. "But that's not what you're most interested in, is it? One night, shortly after my daughter was born, I was on my way to tell Charles about a book I'd located. It told the story of the demon and the hatchet that could kill it. It was late and darker than usual because that night there was no moon.

Las Vegas was very young then and there weren't all the homes and lights that there are today.

"My car had gotten a flat about two blocks from his house and I got out to change the tire. I was only out there about a minute or two when I smelled a repugnant odor. It was like someone took a dozen rotten eggs and threw them in the street beside me. The stench was overpowering, and I struggled to take in a breath, but it was like hitting a wall. I was suffocating. A man approached me, and I was grateful for the help, but that's not why he was there. Helping me was the last thing he wanted to do. I felt a sharp object puncture my gut and the warmth of blood spilling out and soaking my shirt. He stabbed me with a large blade. I collapsed in the street. I don't know how I managed to get up and get to the car, but I did. I drove to Charles' house on the flat tire. When I got there the wound had opened even more and I lay dying on his kitchen floor. Somehow he managed to get me into his car, and we drove out to a small shack in the middle of the desert. There was a man there. He was very old and spoke what sounded like Dutch, but I couldn't be sure. Charles placed me on the floor of his cabin beside the fire burning in a small hearth. He conversed with the man in his native language. The man then came to my side. All I remember is his continuous chant as he passed a knife over my broken body.

197

The flames illuminated the handle, it was crimson with flakes of gold and in the center was carved a circular hex in white, blue, and black. I finally passed out and when I came to I was on his couch all bandaged up. The knife was in the middle of the floor and I was given strict instructions not to touch it. We stayed there through the night and at first light, Charles took me home. On the way, he told me that I would heal, and everything would be alright. But he also told me about the pledge."

"The pledge?"

"Yes. In exchange for my life, I would serve to abolish the demon and protect the chosen. That was the only way that the old man would agree to heal me. They wanted a soldier and they got one. In return, I would live. But there is one term of this agreement that I did not completely understand until the years started passing. I don't grow any older than I was on that night. If I did, then I couldn't uphold my end of the bargain. Until the day comes that the demon is defeated, and the curse is broken, I will remain as you see me. I buried my wife, who I loved more than life itself. I watched as she grew old. I saw the expression she had as she took her last breath. I could never know what she felt watching herself age as I stayed the same. My daughter is an elderly woman, and I will be forced to watch death come for her too. You were right. I am indeed cursed."

"But the chosen one? Have you found them yet?"

"Yes, I have, Noah. And I will finally be able to fulfill the destiny that fate has handed me."

"Well, what are we waiting for? Let's go get them."

"No. We don't have to go anywhere. We already have him."

"Awesome. Okay, where is he?"

"Noah." Jen grabbed his hand and squeezed it gently. "It's you."

"Me? What? No. Jen, you guys have it all confused. I'm not any chosen hero. No way. Have you been sniffing the same crap that you used to knock me out?"

"No, Noah. We're not making this up. It's you."

"She's telling you the truth," Arthur spoke in a gentle voice. "I know this is hard to hear son, but it is true. You are the chosen one."

Noah glared at the two of them. Clearly, they were not only mistaken but genuinely nuts. He couldn't be chosen. He didn't even know about Emma and her family until a couple of weeks ago. No. They had to be wrong.

"Look, Arthur, things have been pretty crazy. So how is it if I'm the chosen one that I didn't even know about this curse until a few weeks ago? And what makes you think it's me anyway? There's a million more logical choices. What about Jon? It would make more sense if it were him."

"No, Noah. It's you. I know it."

"But how? How do you know this?"

"Charles told me. It was written by Bourbon. The man who created the hatchet. The town was cursed, but one small boy escaped their fate that day."

"I know. Thomas Finley."

"That's right. Bourbon found Thomas and gave him two items with clear instructions. Thomas would hold on to them and when he reached adulthood, he would make arrangements to ensure the package made it into the hands of its final destination—you."

"How is that even possible? A man from over a hundred years ago?"

"Bourbon told Thomas he had a vision. The year this would take place and the address to send them to. Thomas waited as instructed and when he was old enough he contacted a local attorney. The items were placed in the box and wrapped.

The law firm would hold the box in their safe until the date designated and then ship it to the specific address in the instructions. Didn't you receive a package recently?"

Noah squirmed. "We did. But it wasn't addressed to me. It was to Thomas Finley, c/o J. Moreno."

"Thomas wasn't given a name, so he used his own. If you inspected the package carefully, you would've noticed that Moreno's name was added. On his deathbed, Thomas had a vision of his own. He saw Moreno's name and a young man. Not knowing anything about the young man, he had his son go to the attorney and add Moreno to the address."

"This still doesn't answer my question. Why me? Why am I the chosen one?"

"Because you are the last living son of Thomas's bloodline before the curse meets its destiny."

"What the hell are you talking about? My family name is Winston, not Finley. And destiny? Do you mean before it seals the town to its death?'

"Yes, before the curse closes the gateway permanently. Noah, Thomas is your great-great-uncle from your mother's bloodline. You are his descendant and kin to his family. They're still alive and captive with the rest of the town. Thomas's father is Matthew Samson's best friend."

"Okay, say I am who you think I am. What's next?"

"First I'll explain the statue."

"No need. Jon already had that covered."

"Then you know it will imprison the demon?"

"I do."

"Did he tell you anything about the necklace?"

"We figured out it belonged to Dallen. Her name and Isaiah 40:29 was inscribed on the back. Jon said it was probably symbolic for protection."

"Yes, the necklace was a present to the girl. Her grandfather gave it to her when she was a child. It had belonged to her mother, who had died from an illness."

"So how did Bourbon get a hold of it?"

"Dallen's brother stole it from his grandfather and gave it to Bourbon. The boy knew his grandfather's rage for the people he blamed for her death."

"And I do what with the necklace?"

"Wear it. It'll help protect you from the demon. Bourbon blessed it with a powerful prayer. Once you put it on, don't take it off. You understand?"

"This is all crazy. I don't feel like anyone's savior."

Jen grabbed his hand and gently rubbed the back of it. "Listen, I was just as surprised as you. Finding out that this boy I've known almost all of my life was the one Arthur has been waiting for all these years, was sort of mind-blowing. But it's true. And now we have to work together to get everyone back and break the curse on the Moreno family. Arthur promised Charles he wouldn't stop until he defeated that disgusting foul abomination."

"You know about the demon too?"

"That night I saw Travis by the church, I smelled it. It was nauseating. I was watching Travis, you know sort of keeping an eye out. I saw what it did, but I was paralyzed from helping him. All I could do was witness it. I know he was pretty shaken, but Arthur didn't want me to say anything to either of you until we were completely sure."

"You've been helping Arthur all along?"

"Yep. Practically since I was old enough to walk."

Arthur interrupted. "I've tried keeping her out of it, but she is extremely stubborn."

"I want to help Arthur find the peace he's been looking for."

Noah exhaled a heavy breath. "I get his life was hard, but he at least had a life."

Arthur stood up and paced around the room for a moment before answering. "Noah, I told you I watched the love of my life grow old and die in my arms. I watched as her eyes looked up at me. She was staring into the same younger man's eyes that she had been looking at for the past forty years. Every day she got a new wrinkle or line, I stayed exactly the same. She stayed by my side and I hers. Toward the end, she was still as beautiful to me as the day I met her, but I could tell she felt it. It broke my heart to have her go through that and I guess part of me was selfish because I needed her and couldn't leave. So, I stayed, and I was a constant reminder of her own mortality. Now all I can think about is one day being with her again.

"I've been very fortunate in many ways. I have been able to see so many changes in the world. And to get to know my great-granddaughter and see her grow into a beautiful young woman is truly the best of all blessings, but it's not my time anymore. It's your time and Jen's and all of your friends."

Noah choked back the tears wanting to break free. He felt so alone. Everything he knew was turned upside down. He couldn't let Jen and Arthur see him cry. The feeling of being useless suffocated him. Emma, Travis, Jon, and now Arthur and Jen. It was too much.

He rubbed his palms on the side of his pants. His chest labored to fill his lungs as he tried calming down.

Okay, they won't hurt Jon just yet. Or at least that's what Arthur thinks. We've got the book with the ritual to summon the demon and the map that leads to the hatchet. Arthur seems to have a small army with the Order of the Protectors so they should be able to get past the Volgeling and their guns. We go to the mountain and find the hatchet. Then we go to the church and summon the demon and kill it. Okay, sounds like a plan.

Unless the Volgeling do win and kill us all. Or we kill them, and the demon kills us, which in turn means the death of everyone else.

Yeah, great plan.

Noah looked up at Arthur and Jen. "I've got a plan. It sucks, but I think it's the only one we got. Tomorrow morning, we go up the mountain and search for the hatchet. Jen, you stay here so in case something happens you can let Trav and Emma know."

Jen frowned.

"Yeah, I know. You'd rather go with us and risk death, but we need you here." Noah laughed to himself. Jen is really a whole different person than he thought. "Arthur, we're going to need as many Protectors as you can get. Those Volgeling are pretty ruthless, which I'm sure you know, and when we go up to the mountain you can bet they will be there to stop us."

"Don't worry. We have a vast number of pledges on our side. I've been recruiting for this day for many years and each generation of families has pledged allegiance to our cause. We'll have a sufficient number to defend ourselves."

"Good. Now that leaves the summoning of the demon. It stated in the book that the ritual needs to be performed right at dusk in the same place that they are able to cross over. That's at the entrance to the church. Arthur, you'll read the chant and when the demon appears, I'll kill it with the hatchet. Then you can banish it to the statue." Noah acknowledged the uncertainty in Arthur's eyes. "I know—it's a ridiculously obvious plan but it's all we got. Unless there's something I'm missing?"

"No. It's just that after all these years you've summed it up so simply. It sounds quite laughable."

"Yeah, well, try not to laugh too hard. We haven't succeeded yet."

Arthur faintly smiled and squeezed his shoulder before walking away.

Jen got up and sat next to Noah. "This means a lot to him. He's been at it for so many years."

"I know. Jen. I get it. I do."

They began putting the details in place. They would start by going to the church at dusk to tell Travis and Emma everything. Emma could explain to Matthew and the rest of the town what was about to happen. Afterward, Jen would go with him to gather everything they needed for the ritual. Some of the items were a bit uncommon, but she was sure they could get most of what they needed from the Psychic Eye. A store specializing in Wiccan practices, they were stocked with the best selection of herbs and natural remedies.

Arthur worked on the strategy for their defenses once they were on the mountain. He stayed behind with his men to map things out. Jen drove herself and Noah over to the church just in time for Emma and the others to crossover. Travis, still groggy from the journey, stiffened his lip when he saw Jen.

"Noah, what the hell is she doing here?"

"Easy, Trav. Sit down, you're still pretty shaky."

"Dude. I don't wanna sit down. Just tell me what's going on."

Noah grabbed Emma's hand, much to the dismay of Ezekiel, who had narrowed his eyes, but Noah pretended not to notice. He figured they had much bigger issues to discuss in a very short time and worrying about whether it was proper to hold her hand was not a priority. He sat them all down and as quickly as he could, he explained everything that had happened in the past twenty-four hours. Then Jen jumped in and mapped out the details for the next night. Noah studied the expression on Travis's face.

"Trav, can we talk for a sec?" Noah waved for him to follow.

The boys walked around the church to the back of the property.

"Do you have any reservations about our plan?" Noah asked.

"I just need for this to work. Sure, I'm freaked out. But it's less about the demon and more about if I get stuck there permanently. I told you, it'll drive me insane."

"You're getting out of there—you all are. Arthur has like a hundred guys ready to go and fight and we have the map with the location of the hatchet. Jen and I will find all the ingredients we need. This damn demon doesn't stand a chance. He's gonna be dust by tomorrow night, I promise. You just got to hold on for one more night. Okay?"

"Damn, I never thought I'd say, this but if it doesn't work, don't come looking for me the next night." Travis kicked the dirt.

"Dude, if this doesn't work I won't be able to. I'll be dead."

"Wow, some pep talk. You're a real confidence builder. Well, if it does work, do you think Jen would go out with me? She's really hot in a Buffy kind of way."

"Really? That's your takeaway? We might die and you're thinking about a girl?"

Travis grinned, but Noah knew his friend. He was scared. They both were.

Chapter Seventeen

Noah sat in the passenger seat of Arthur's car discussing their plans for the day, while Jen closed her eyes in the back. They were traveling down Charleston Boulevard on their way to his house. The conversation hit a lull and he gazed out the window. The neon light above a popular burger hangout wouldn't come on until dark.

Noah sighed. He and Travis practically lived there during their high school days. It felt good for just a moment to think of something so normal like chilling with friends over a burger and fries. Everything had been turned upside down lately and it was about to get worse. He and Arthur were planning a trip up the mountain first thing in the morning and he couldn't help but wonder if it'd be his last hike. Arthur guaranteed the Order of Protectors would be following them every step of the way, but not even the watchful eye of warriors sworn to give their life for others, was enough to ease Noah's anxiety.

Noah needed to get some of Jon's books that he'd hidden in his room the day before. With all the craziness, they figured everyone would center their search around Jon's office and not Noah's house. He hated risking exposure to his parents, but they needed a quick fix and that was it. Arthur could place a protection spell on the house until morning, so they decided that was the best plan.

When they arrived, a note on the fridge from Noah's mom eased the tension of a secret mission and gave them room to breathe. Her sister had invited them to her lake house for a few days and she thought it would be good for his dad to get away from Vegas and the doctors for a while. She'd tried to reach him on his cell, but it had gone to voicemail, and she assumed he was at work. Noah gave a sigh of relief. One less thing to worry about. He kept wondering how he was going to explain why Jen and Arthur were spending the night. Now it seemed he was off the hook.

"Arthur, you and Jen can stay in the guest room. My mom always leaves the bed made up and ready in case family decides to surprise us and come to town." Noah rolled his eyes. It seemed everyone who needed to get away thought Vegas was the place to do it. They would come at a moment's notice and knock on their door. His parents were nice about it. Noah was less forgiving.

Arthur was exhausted, so after he placed the protection spell, he went to lie down while Jen and Noah grabbed something to eat in the kitchen. His mom had left him some dinners in the refrigerator ready to pop in the microwave. While he was waiting he couldn't help but stare at Jen. So strange to think that he had no clue all this time who she really was.

"After I finish eating I'm gonna go up to the store for the supplies. Keep an eye on Arthur for me okay?"

Noah nodded. "I will, but something tells me Arthur is definitely capable of taking care of himself."

"Yeah, I know. But lately, he seems to be a little restless. I'm not sure if it's because we're so close to ending this and he can hopefully get some peace, or if this is finally getting to him after all these years. Either way, watch him, okay?"

"Will do."

Noah attacked the nuked frozen beef and bean burrito like it was a gourmet meal from Wolfgang Puck's restaurant in the MGM. When they were finished, Jen got up and washed her plate. Setting it on the rack beside the sink to dry, she grabbed her purse from the counter and slung it over her shoulder.

"Hey, you sure about going out on your own?" Noah knitted a brow.

"I'm not alone." She pulled out a black handgun from her purse. "I'm taking a friend."

Noah just shook his head and chuckled. After she left he sat in the kitchen for a while thinking about Jon and Travis. He wished he knew for sure that no one had harmed Jon and that Arthur was right. But being in the dark and not knowing was driving him crazy. Jon had a wife and a son coming. And if he wasn't already dead, he would be shortly because of the curse. Travis had been his best friend since they were kids, and he couldn't imagine life without him. And then there was Emma. She had spent over a hundred years damned to just existing. She deserved to live. The whole town did. They couldn't fail. He couldn't fail. Tomorrow when they went up the mountain, he knew he might have to do things that he never thought he would be capable of.

But now, with all his friends and the girl he loved depending on him, he would have to make choices. And he knew given the situation, no matter what, he would choose them.

They woke up with the first light of dawn, it was New Years Eve—one day until the New Year. They checked and rechecked everything they needed.

If there was an altercation with the Volgeling then they wanted to make damn sure they were ready. Noah had a backpack that he was loading everything into. Climbing the mountain would be easier with both of his hands free. Arthur gave him a 40-caliber handgun and a large hunting knife. Noah had never fired a gun, so they gave him a crash course, which did little to build his confidence. He hoped he didn't have to use it—but he would.

Arthur was armed too, and it shocked Noah when he saw him tuck some grenades in his jacket pocket. He knew they were heading into danger, but the grenades weren't something he expected. He didn't question it though. He figured Arthur knew what he was doing after all these years and it gave him an added sense of security knowing they were ready, or at the very least, armed with a small arsenal.

Jen drove them to the base of the mountain. As they said their goodbyes, she sighed. Noah figured he had a fairly good idea of what she was thinking. She had wanted to go too, but they needed someone to stay behind in case they didn't make it down. Jen half-heartedly volunteered because she knew he was the chosen one and had to go. She was right.

The map had indicated a small cave halfway up the northwest side of the mountain. Once inside they needed to find a large red stone about the size of a loaf of bread.

Directly underneath was where the hatchet was buried. It sounded so easy. It was so close all these years and yet no one had been able to get to it. This time he hoped it would be different. It had to be.

They passed the last row of houses that were built on the mountain and started hiking towards the north. The way the map read, it should take them about an hour before they reached the cave. While they were walking, Noah looked around. "Arthur, I thought you said your men would be with us. I haven't seen anyone."

Arthur smirked. "Oh, they're here. Trust me, if we need them they will show themselves. They are just watching and keeping an eye out for danger, but they are within earshot of us."

Noah scanned the desert landscape straining his eyes to catch a glimpse of someone who might be tucked behind a bush or some dried brush. He hoped Arthur was right and they were there. Otherwise, this would end very badly. As they climbed, he noticed paths that were cut out in the dirt. He figured some off-roaders must come up here with their dirt bikes and ride the trail. On the other side was Lake Mead, and it would probably be fun navigating through here if you didn't have the threat of impending death hanging over your head.

This mountain was so different than the ones he had seen in California on his last family vacation. The California mountains were green with grass and trees. But the desert mountains were shades of brown, tan and sometimes even gray. They held a mystery about them, looking void of any real form of life but all the while bursting with various species of small animals and desert plants. They could look very gloomy or they could appear serene, depending on your perception. Noah always found them to be serene. They had been his solace on many frenzied days. And even today, facing unknown danger, the mountain gave him a sense of calm.

They were about fifty minutes into their climb when Arthur stopped. He pivoted around, scouring the surroundings. Noah started to say something, but Arthur raised his hand for him to keep quiet. He unsnapped the holster that was strapped to his side and withdrew his handgun. Noah didn't see anything but took the knife out of his jacket pocket and stood with his back to Arthur. He figured if anyone was coming they would be able to see in every direction. They waited in prep mode, ready to strike. But after a couple of minutes, Arthur tapped him on the shoulder and nodded it was okay to go on.

No sooner had they taken a step that he saw someone or something, pass by the right side of him. He turned, opting to grab the gun this time.

Arthur had already drawn his pistol again and was poised waiting to shoot. Noah heard a pop and dropped to the ground. He remembered that sound from the attack at the church. The Volgeling were here, and they were shooting at them. There was no place to hide. Noah bobbed his head up but he couldn't figure out where they were coming from. He heard it again. Pow, pow, pow. Arthur pushed him further down to the ground and covered him. Given the pledge, Arthur was in no immediate danger, but Noah was a different story. Bullets would definitely do their job on his fragile flesh.

They belly crawled along the parched terrain and Noah tightened up when a new blast of shots came from the opposite direction. The Protectors must be here. Arthur was right. They had gone about twenty feet when Arthur told him to get up and run toward the cave.

Noah hesitated. "Aren't you coming?"

"I'll be right behind you. Now go."

Noah ran in the direction Arthur had pointed out. The cave wasn't visible from where he was and he silently asked the universe to lead him to the right place. He could hear more gunfire and shouting but didn't stop to look back. He figured their best bet was for him to reach the cave and find the hatchet.

The next thing he knew he was knocked off his feet and plummeting to the ground. The impact had forced all the air from his lungs, and he struggled to expand his chest. There was a sharp pain in the small of his back and he could see the outline of a husky man hovering over him with a large, serrated knife in his hand. The stranger's lips were moving but Noah was too disoriented to distinguish what he was saying. The man clasped the knife with both hands and raised it up in the air. Noah fought to gain back control and raise his arms up to block the knife.

He regained his hearing and stiffened when he realized the man's chant. "Die so that he may live. Die so that he may live."

The Volgeling sliced the air with the knife trying to pierce Noah's chest, but he and the blade nicked his side instead. Gasping, Noah shoved his attacker with his legs and the man fell, slamming his back on nearby rocks. As Noah stumbled to his feet, Arthur came running between the two of them and he heard a loud pop. The man lay still, and a river of red streamed from his chest. Noah stared, unable to turn away.

"He would've killed you without a thought," Arthur said.

"He almost did." Noah removed his bloody hand from his wound.

Arthur inspected the gash. "Hang on."

Pulling off his jacket and layered button-up, he wound the shirt several times into a makeshift bandage and tied it around Noah's waist, protecting the wound. Putting his jacket back on, he inspected his work.

"That should slow down the bleeding for now. Can you walk?"

"Yeah, but it hurts like a mother."

"Come on, we haven't much time. Things are getting bad out there and we need to find the cave and get you home."

Noah nodded. Arthur took the map out and pointed to a mark where the cave was supposed to be. The two men hiked over a small ridge which led them straight to their destination. Noah looked down at his throbbing side. The light blue cotton had turned purple.

A pungent odor tickled his nostrils. "Do you smell it?"

The two men winced.

"The demon is coming. Noah, we're doomed if it corners us inside this cave. You go look for the hatchet. I'll stay here and see if I can distract it."

"No, Arthur. I think we need to stay together. I know you think you're indestructible or something, but this is a demon. He could probably rip you to shreds, pledge or no pledge."

"I'll be okay. Besides, you're the one bleeding all over my shirt. Go. Find that damn thing so we can get the hell out of here."

Noah hesitantly stumbled away. He took out his flashlight and began scouring the ground. The further inside he went the more nervous he felt. What if he couldn't find it? What if the demon killed Arthur? What if he bled out in this cave and no one ever found his body?

Stop thinking and keep looking.

He felt the ground shake and fine dust settled into his eyes. He put the flashlight on the ground and brushed it away with a bandana he had stuffed in his back pocket. When he was certain he had cleared out all the debris he crouched down to pick up the light. About six inches in front of him was a large red stone. He carefully removed the stone and set it aside. He pulled a small gardening shovel from his backpack and pounded the sharp tip into the hard desert floor. Each swing of the tool stretched his gaping flesh sending waves of nausea to his gut.

He kept going.

Several inches down he heard a clunk from the shovel. Furiously, Noah pushed the dirt away revealing the lid of a small, wooden box.

He quickly dug around the sides and then brushed the remaining dirt away. Lifting it from its grave he placed it on the ground beside him. There was a simple piece of rope holding the lid shut. Noah took the knife out, cut the rope, and opened the box, revealing the prize of the spellbound hatchet.

He couldn't believe it. So many people had died trying to find it and here it was in his hands. This was the key to saving everyone. He quickly wrapped it up in the bandana and tucked it in his backpack. Holding his side, he ambled back toward the mouth of the cave. The closer he got the more his eyes and nose burned from the stench.

The demon was uncomfortably close. He only hoped they could get out in one piece. As he came around the last turn, his flashlight dimmed, and he smacked it with his hand. It flickered before regaining a full beam. Noah held the torch in front of him to light a path but gasped in horror when he saw Arthur dangling in midair, his arms wailing to fend off the invisible enemy.

The stink forced the churning acids from Noah's stomach into the back of his throat. Coughing, he spewed hot bile onto the desert floor.

Peering up at the horror in front him, Arthur was losing his battle. The demon was slowly crushing the air from his lungs.

"Arthur!" Noah rushed toward him, but Arthur put his hand up. In an instant, Arthur dropped to the ground. The dirt on the desert floor parted, sending dust swirling around the entryway, blocking Noah's vision. The stench grew closer; the demon was coming toward him.

Noah collapsed in exhaustion. Arthur reached into his pocket and grabbed a grenade. With command, he called out, "Jedediah Smith!"

Noah covered his ears as a deep roar shook the ground beneath him. He watched as Arthur bent down and grabbed a large handful of sand from the floor of the cave.

"Noah. Listen to me. When I throw this sand, I want you to see which way is clear and then run like hell. Can you do that, can you run?"

Noah looked confused. "I…I don't know. I think it's blocking my way. I can feel it's breath. Arthur, it's right here."

"Noah, I know you're hurting and scared. But son, you need to get up. We're leaving here right now. Okay?"

"Okay." Noah placed his palms in the sand and pushed himself up. Teetering, he fought to gain his balance.

"Get ready!' Arthur called out. "Now!" Arthur threw the large handful of sand in the air. "Run, Noah! Run!"

Noah took a few strides but stopped. He was paralyzed with fear. Standing in front of him, uncloaked by the loose sand, was the demon. Its silhouette was similar to a man, but about seven or eight feet tall. Pieces of charred flesh sparsely covered the huge muscles on its arms and legs. Its feet were infested with large bumps resembling tumors and its skull was mainly compromised of knotted bone with skin stretching to mimic a face. Its mouth was filled with razor-sharp teeth and a brown mucous-like substance was dripping from its misshapen gape. Noah grabbed the wall of the cave to steady himself. If this really was Jedediah, there was nothing human left in him.

"Damn it, kid, snap out of it and get the hell out of here!"

Noah looked up and saw Arthur waving him on, a grenade in his other hand. He noticed a clear path to the left of the demon and darted for it. The beast lunged for him, but Noah managed to dodge out of the way of its clutches and kept running.

Arthur shouted for him to keep going and as Noah passed by, Arthur followed. The light of the opening grew closer and when they were both clear, Arthur spun around and threw the grenade right in front of the pursuing demon. The two men dove to the dirt and covered their heads. There was a loud boom and a landslide of boulders and sand streamed down covering the opening.

Arthur scrambled to his feet and wrapped his arm around Noah, hoisting him up and guiding him to the base of the mountain.

Chapter Eighteen

Arthur kept his eyes on the surrounding area watching for any signs of the Volgeling, but no one bothered them. When they finally reached the bottom, Jen was waiting in the car about a hundred feet away. Seeing her great-grandfather holding up Noah, she leaped from the car and ran to help.

"What the hell happened? Oh jeez, there's so much blood."

"Jen." Arthur glared. "It looks worse than what it is."

"Yeah, it barely hurts now," Noah said in a raspy voice.

"Good try. Let's get you in the car." Jen firmly grasped his other arm.

After they lay Noah down in the back seat, Jen sped off and drove straight to the Winston's house. Once they were there, Arthur thoroughly cleaned and properly bandaged the wound.

Noah lay on the couch and Jen walked in with three glasses and a bottle of Jack Daniels.

"I figured we could all use this, especially you." She nodded to Noah.

"I could have a drink—or ten." He laughed and then winced. "Damn, it hurts."

"You want something for the pain? I have connections." Arthur pulled his phone from his back pocket.

"No thanks. I have my painkiller right here." Noah held up his glass of bourbon.

"What happened up there?" asked Jen.

Arthur told her a condensed version of the encounter and poured another glass of Jack.

"You both got lucky."

"It's not dead, is it?" Noah's gaze traveled to Arthur.

"No. We only bought some time. The rock will only hold it for a short while."

"We need to postpone our plans." Jen tucked her hair behind her ears. "Noah's in no condition to fight."

"Forget it. It's happening. You heard Arthur, it looks worse than what it is. It doesn't matter what happened today. I have to kill this thing or my friends, the town and who knows who else will die."

"Then we do battle tonight as planned," Arthur stated.

"Have you two lost your minds? I'm all in for some demon knock down but this is reckless. If Noah falls on the battlefield, and there's a good chance he will, we'll be even more vulnerable than we are now."

Noah shook his head. "That thing isn't gonna wait for me to heal. It's gonna keep coming until it gets what it wants. But we're not letting that happen."

Arthur told Noah the Volgeling would probably bring Jon to the church for leverage. Their main objective was to protect their demon. They'd anticipate the summoning and probably count on Noah backing off to save Jon's life. But the only way he could help Jon was to succeed.

It was getting close to dusk and they wanted to be there a few minutes early to have ample time to set up. Jen had gathered the rest of the ingredients that they needed while they were on the mountain and she packed everything in a small leather bag that hung across her chest. Looking up, she locked eyes with Arthur.

"What's up?" she asked.

"I mean this, Granddaughter: if things go sour, you don't look back and you get the hell out of there. I know you think you need to watch out for me, but I'm the one who's immortal right now. Not you."

"Understood."

Noah slowly got to his feet. Reaching for his hoodie that was slung over the back of the couch, he slipped it on and zipped it up. The thick material felt like an extra barrier shielding his wound and the pain was steadily reducing to a manageable ache.

"Noah, hold on for a moment." Arthur pulled Dallen's necklace from his front pocket and handed it to Noah.

"How do you have that? It was in Jon's office." Noah stiffened his lip.

Arthur cocked his head. "Do you really need an explanation?"

Noah sighed.

"Now put this on and whatever happens, do not remove it."

They loaded everything into Arthur's car and drove to the church. They opted to park a block away from the structure in case the Volgeling had come early to the party.

Cautiously they trekked to where Noah hoped would be the beginning of the end and the rebirth for everyone involved.

As they approached the grounds, Noah noticed four men standing with handguns just inside the gate. One of them was pointing his gun down toward the ground. As they got closer, he could see it was Jon staring down at the barrel. Arthur narrowed his eyes and Noah knew what he meant. Focus. When they reached the property lines, the picture became clearer. Directly behind the Volgeling was a group of Protectors. They were carrying guns too and they had them pointed at the four men. Arthur nodded to what appeared to be the leader. It looked like things were going relatively smoothly, Noah thought. That was until he realized there was an army of additional Volgeling and Protectors surrounding the perimeter of the church. Not good.

Jen set her bag down on the ground in front of Arthur and began removing the supplies. Laying out everything they needed, each one grabbed a pistol and extra clips.

"Everybody good?" Jen asked.

Arthur nodded.

"What about you, Noah? You feeling okay?"

"I'll feel better when this shit is over, but yeah. I'm good."

Arthur needed to start a small fire so he could put all the ingredients into a black cast iron pot and let them boil. Once they boiled and smoke rose he could recite the chant from his aunt's book, and using its name, summon the demon. Timing would be everything. Emma, Travis and the boys would be coming through at the same time and they had only precious minutes to succeed. They all knew the plan, it was explained to them the night before, but what they didn't know was what they were dealing with. Up until earlier that day neither did Noah. But now he had seen the demon for what it was, and it paralyzed him.

"How long before the demon shows?" asked Noah.

"After I finish summoning it, only seconds."

"Great because…" Noah felt the poke of cold steel on his neck. "Fuck."

Arthur and Jen quickly turned. Two of the Volgeling had branched off from their strategic positions and had their guns focused on Noah.

Jen swiftly pivoted and called out to Noah, "Drop!" She swept her leg around and into the back of the knees of the startled Volgeling, knocking him to the ground. A quick thump to the head with the butt of her pistol and the man was out cold.

Arthur attacked the second gunman, punching him in the head several times until his gun fell to the ground. Wrapping his right arm around the man's neck, he squeezed. Both men fell to the ground as the Volgeling fought furiously for his life, but he was no match for Arthur's years of hate and frustration. Holding onto him with a vice grip, Arthur stole the man's last breath.

Noah's gaze traveled from Arthur to the lifeless body. "Is he dead?"

Arthur released a heavy breath. "Yes."

Noah turned away. He knew this was a real possibility but imagining it and seeing it was an entirely different thing.

"Hey, we need finish this." Jen handed Arthur the pot. "Noah, help me start the fire. Bunch up the dried brush and kindling we brought."

Noah did as instructed, and Jen lit the flame.

Arthur placed all the ingredients in the pot and soon after the smoke began to rise.

He opened the book and chanted words completely foreign to Noah. The temperature plummeted, chilling the air and creating a blustery wind. Noah peered up at the sky; a ferocious funnel spun above them. Expanding both in speed and size, its roar intensified as lightning sawed through the sky, ushering in the thunderous crackle of light. The ground rumbled, and Noah struggled to gain his footing. Using the moment to his advantage, Jon shoved one of the Volgeling to the ground and the Protectors moved in, surrounding Jon as he ran toward his friends.

The Volgeling attacked.

Jen and Noah stayed by Arthur's side, guns drawn. When Jon reached them, they handed him a pistol.

"You okay?" Noah asked Jon.

"I've been better." Jon grinned. "Who's she?"

"Jen, this is Jon, Jon…Jen."

"Hey." Jen tightened the grip on her gun. "Let's surround Arthur, this fucking chaos is about to crash in on us."

Noah peered around. Men were falling to the ground and more kept coming. Like ants on the ground after a rainfall, their numbers felt endless.

"How come no one's shooting?" Noah asked.

"A fight on a construction site is one thing. Gunfire brings too much attention. The police would be here in minutes. They won't fire until they have to. The Volgeling won't risk getting their precious demon master angry."

Jon eyed Arthur and turned to Noah. "The guy from the plane?"

"Yup. I'll fill you in after we don't die."

"I can wait."

The thunderous boom above them rang in Noah's head and he struggled to cover his ears.

Arthur reached out and grabbed Noah's arm. "It's trying to distract you," he shouted. "That's the reason for the explosive show. Don't pay any attention, it will stop soon."

The moment Arthur said his final sentence, the wind stopped. Noah uncovered his ears and dropped his shoulders. He cast a gaze toward the church doorway and saw Emma and Travis, then Ezekiel and Henry. All the men halted. The nauseating odor permeated around him and Noah knew—the demon.

The beast was standing in the center of the front property of the church when he turned around.

The overwhelming stench brought a few of the men to their knees as they spewed up the last contents of their stomachs. He looked back at Emma and Travis, their rounded eyes frozen in horror. Ezekiel had grabbed Henry and shoved him into the doorway, sending him back to the other side. The demon turned and clumped toward Emma.

Noah grabbed the hatchet from his backpack and ran for the demon, approaching from behind. He picked up speed and threw his full body weight onto the back of the monstrosity. Slamming his injured side against its putrid flesh, Noah ignored the heat rising from his wound. Clinging with his left arm around the neck of the beast, he raised the hatchet.

Merely inches away from its charred nape, Noah found himself at the mercy of a Volgeling. The depraved man had gripped the hood of Noah's jersey and yanked. Both men fell to the ground. Ezekiel raced toward Noah, and Travis took Emma's hand and they both ran to Arthur. Ezekiel slipped a large hunting knife from his belt and snuck up behind the Volgeling, pulled back his head and slit his throat. Noah was released from his clutches and redirected his sites on the demon. The beast swung one of its powerful arms and knocked Travis clear across the lawn to the other side of the property. Arthur attempted to seize the demon, but a thrash to the head and Arthur's fate was the desert floor.

Emma stood motionless. Tears streamed down her cheeks, as she clutched her chest.

"Emma!" Noah cried out.

The demon raised one hand in the air and Emma lifted off the ground. Her body shook violently as her eyes rolled to the back of her head.

Jen pounced at the deformed beast, repeatedly shooting it in the back, while Noah sprinted to reach Emma. An iron-hot poker seared his side and he glanced down. Vital fluid seeped through the bandage, dampening his t-shirt and hoodie. Wincing, he kept moving.

Attacking from the front, Noah threw himself into the oozing, charred flesh of the beast's chest. He raised the hatchet and sliced through the air, missing the beast by inches. The demon wrapped its arms around him and tried to squeeze the air from his lungs, but Dallen's necklace grazed the demon's chest. The beast screeched in agony, releasing Noah from its grip.

Noah quickly scrambled to his feet, took the hatchet, and made several chops to the demon's neck. The demon collapsed to the ground and Noah stood above, wielding the final blow that severed its head. Emma fell to the ground and gasped for air.

A deafening boom was followed by a moment of stillness. Arthur quickly retrieved the golden statue from his bag and recited the prayer to seal the demon for all eternity.

With the flash of a brilliant light, the lifeless beast was gone.

Collapsing next to her, Noah took Emma into his arms. Ezekiel and Travis scrambled to their feet and ran toward them. Jon and Arthur followed. The Volgeling, realizing their master had been defeated, fled. The Protectors exchanged a few words with Arthur before their quiet exit.

Noah caressed her hair and gently kissed her cheek.

She buried her head into his chest and sobbed.

"It didn't work," she whispered.

"What do you mean?" Noah was confused.

"The curse. Where are they? I don't see anyone. They didn't make it."

"It must have worked. Look." Noah pointed to the indigo sky. "Dusk is over and you're all okay."

Emma wiped the tears from her eyes and peered up at the shadow of the mountain.

"Arthur, what do you...wait. Listen. Do you hear it?" A faint buzz hummed from the frame of the church. "It's coming from the gateway," Noah said excitedly.

"Oh jeez, what is that?" Travis winced and turned his head.

The darkness parted, revealing a bright orange and yellow beam melting over the midnight sky. Like the closing of a door, in a moment it was gone, taking the painful buzz with it.

"Emma?"

They all turned toward the doorway of the church. There stood Matthew, his wife, and Henry. Emma ran to them and embraced her little brother with a tight hug. One by one the townspeople came through until every last person had crossed.

Jen walked over and bumped shoulders with Travis.

"So I guess we're kind of like heroes," he said with a smile.

"I guess we are." Jen's hand brushed against his. "It feels pretty good."

"Awesome."

Matthew approached Noah and extended his hand. "We have so much to thank you for. You have our lifelong gratitude."

Noah nodded.

He put his hand out for Emma and she interlaced her fingers with his. Matthew furrowed his brow for a moment before softening and giving a slight sway of his head.

Emma lowered her gaze to his bloodied side. "This does not look good."

He unzipped his hoodie and partially pulled up his t-shirt. Examining the wound, he faintly smiled. "I'll be okay, the bleeding just about stopped. Although sitting would be good about now," he crinkled his nose.

She helped Noah to one of the boulders and sat down.

After a few moments, he turned and gazed into her eyes. Gently holding her face, he brushed her hair away. There was so much he wanted to tell her and show her.

Dawn would be theirs.

EPILOGUE

VALENTINE'S DAY

It had been nearly two months since Noah had broken the curse and saved Emma and the town from perishing. Emma's family and the rest of the town had settled in a rural area of Las Vegas on five acres of land that Arthur had purchased nearly fifty years ago. He'd planned for their arrival, or at least hoped they would get the chance to live again. Over the years he had small homes built on the property, and the bungalows that had been completed were enough for all the surviving families to live comfortably.

Ten days after the altercation, and freedom of the townspeople, Arthur passed away in his sleep with a gentle smile on his face. Noah couldn't help but feel happy for the man who had given so much to help so many. He had finally gotten the peace he'd yearned for. He liked to think of Arthur seeing his wife again, all the pain washed away by their embrace.

Jon had a huge party at Sunset Gardens for his 40th birthday. There must have been two hundred of his closest friends and family, complete with a live band and open bar.

The topper of the evening, however, was when his wife went into labor just as they were cutting the cake. Arthur Jon Moreno weighed 7lbs and 6oz and had as much hair on his head as his dad.

The drive out to see Emma took about forty-five minutes, but he didn't mind. Noah stole away every chance he could get just for them to be able to sit and talk. Even though this was the twenty-first century, Matthew Samson was a nineteenth-century man. He was concerned for his daughter out in a world that had long passed them by. Noah had not been allowed to take Emma off the property since they moved there. Most of their nights were spent with her family. Once in a while, they would go for a walk, but only in the confines of the immediate area.

But tonight, it was going to be different. For the first time, he was going to be able to take Emma on a real date. After much coaxing and help from Jon, he finally convinced Matthew to let her go to dinner with him at an actual restaurant. Jon explained that this would help her become accustomed to this new time. He reasoned that all their children would be growing up in a very different world than he and his wife had, and they would eventually have to let them experience things. If he kept them sheltered away then it was like they had never lifted the curse and were still stuck in the abyss. Matthew agreed with some grumbling.

Noah didn't mind. Spending one hour alone with Emma was enough to make his heartbeat wildly in his chest and his stomach flip. To have an entire evening was mind-blowing.

He had gotten off work early and picked up a dozen white roses for her. He knew it was Valentine's Day and red roses were the thing to buy, but Emma preferred white ones. She loved how graceful and simple they were. A couple of days before he had gone into one of the jewelry shops in the mall and bought her a necklace. It was white gold with a small diamond key and heart dangling from it. She would hold his heart and the key to it forever. Okay, it sounded a bit corny, but it wouldn't to Emma. He knew it was something she would totally get and love.

He went home to take a quick shower and put on some fresh clothes. His mom and dad were getting ready to go out too. His dad had made a reservation at one of the upscale steak houses on the Strip. He had been doing better with his treatments and putting some weight back on. So, they were going out for a double celebration. Noah watched his mom put the finishing touches on her hair before leaving. She looked so much happier than she had these past few months.

"You look really pretty, Mom." He flashed her a smile.

"Thank you." She gave him a tight mom hug. "You going out tonight?"

"Yeah. I've got a date." He hadn't told his parents about Emma just yet. "I'm picking up Travis and Jen and then we're heading over to Emma's."

"Travis and Jen, huh?"

"Yeah, they got together a couple of weeks ago. He really likes her."

"That's good. I like Jen. Maybe she can knock a little sense into Travis and tame him a little."

Noah laughed. "Oh, I'm sure if anyone can tame Travis, it'll be Jen."

"So. Who is this Emma?" His mother had a little smirk on her face.

"You'll meet her soon enough. We're taking it slow. Okay?"

"Alright. Have a good time and drive safe."

"I will." Noah leaned over and kissed his mom on the cheek and then headed to the shower.

When he was dressed and ready to go, he drove over to Travis's first to pick him up. When he got there his friend was waiting nervously at the curb.

He had a dozen red roses and a box of Godiva chocolates in his hand. After he was in the car he slumped down in his seat and sighed.

"Dude, what's wrong?" Noah was confused. Travis had been so stoked about dating Jen and he was so excited about Valentine's Day all week. Now he was mopey.

"I should have bought her jewelry. You got Emma that cool necklace. I think Jen's gonna be disappointed."

"No, Trav. Dude, Jen's not like that. She will love the flowers and the candy. I got Emma the necklace because everything for her is so different now. I wanted her to have something that she could look at every day and know everything would be okay. Believe me, Jen is not expecting anything like that yet. You're good."

"You really think so?"

"Yeah, I do."

"Okay, thanks."

They picked up Jen from her house and then headed away from town. She and Travis sat in the back seat where he gave her the roses and chocolate. Noah peeked through the rear-view mirror and chuckled at the Cheshire cat grin splashed across her face.

He was glad they had found each other. It was still light out and the sun beating down into the car made it toasty and comfortable. Noah's mind drifted over the past few months and how so much had changed. He was excited about what the future might bring and content in knowing that everyone he loved was in a pretty good place.

When they reached the Samson house, Matthew was waiting outside. He motioned for Noah to join him and they sat down in two lawn chairs that were in the front garden.

Matthew cleared his throat. "Noah, I want you to know that although we are very grateful for everything that you and your friends have done, we are still very much rooted in our ways."

"I understand."

"Do you?"

"Yes. You want to be sure Emma's safe with me. She is, I promise you."

"And if for one moment you forget that promise…"

"I won't."

Matthew stood up, nodded, and went into the house.

Noah walked back toward the car. Travis and Jen had gotten out and were leaning up against the hood.

"Dude. What did he say?"

"Oh, you know, the usual. I have a shotgun and it would be really easy to bury you here where no one would find your body...that sort of thing."

"For real?."

"Nah." He laughed.

Noah heard the door open and turned around. There was Emma. Her chestnut hair loosely cascaded down her shoulders, highlighted by the sun's rays revealing streaks of gold and honey. His heart skipped a beat and he gasped. She was so beautiful. Jen had taken her shopping for the occasion and they had found the perfect dress. Matthew had been difficult at first about the length but with a lot of fast-talking from Jen, they were able to settle on just below the knee.

Emma had picked a vivid emerald, green that illuminated the brilliant color of her eyes. He approached her and gently clasped his hand in hers. Opening the car door for her, she slid into the front seat. He shut the door and ran around to the other side. After he was in and buckled, he took her hand again and drew it to his lips, kissing along her velvety skin.

Emma reached out and placed her hand over his and he caressed the side of her cheek with his tingling fingers. They locked eyes and she smiled.

"Are you excited about tonight?"

"I could think of nothing else all day."

"You look so beautiful."

Emma's cheeks glowed. "Thank you."

"Are things starting to feel more normal?"

"It has been exciting, troubling, but never one day since we returned do I regret living to see this strange and wonderful century. The years of isolation have given all of us a gift we could have never imagined."

"It must have been agony, all that time lost in the abyss."

"Not lost."

"What do you mean?" Noah blinked.

"My mother says our time there was like a spool of thread."

"Thread?"

"Yes. When you pull the end it unravels, but yet it remains attached. We were just…unthreaded."

About the Author

Originally from New York, I currently reside in Nevada. Writing Young Adult paranormal, I find my inspiration from events that have been in my life for as long as I can remember.

Inheriting my sensitivity to the supernatural from my family, they continue to be an endless source of vision.

www.vickiannbush.com

Also By Vicki-Ann Bush

Alex McKenna and the Geranium Deaths
Alex McKenna & The Geranium Deaths – Audible Edition
Alex McKenna & The Academy of Souls – Audible Edition
Alex McKenna & A Winter's Night - Audible Edition

Stand-alone titles
Ophelia
The Garden of Two
Saving A Life
The Queen of IT
Winslow Willow the Woodland Fairy

Short Stories
The Joshua Tree
Surviving

COMING 2024
The Darkest Light - YA Paranormal Romance
A teen angel, a tormented demon, and a bond that can't be broken

Liminal Space - Sci-Fi
"All that we see or seem is but a dream within a dream."
- Edgar Allan Poe